The Witching Woman

The Witching Woman

Sarah Vern

ROBERT HALE · LONDON

First published in Great Britain 2005

ISBN 0 7090 7915 X

Robert Hale Limited
Clerkenwell House
Clerkenwell Green
London EC1R 0HT

2 4 6 8 10 9 7 5 3 1

Typeset in 11/14 pt Palatino
by Derek Doyle & Associates, Shaw Heath.
Printed in Great Britain by St Edmundsbury Press,
Bury St Edmunds, Suffolk.
Bound by Woolnough Bookbinding Ltd.

PART I

TORA

CHAPTER ONE

ALEXANDER McNair first saw the island of Tora in 1896 and his initial impressions suggested that his banishment there would prove to be even more punitive than he had imagined.

Peering over the undulating side of the boat, he could see nothing about this dark blob of land which was even faintly enticing. Signs of any kind of civilization were as yet invisible; a thick collar of mist obliterated the mountainous peak that gave the island its name; and the choppy grey sea, choking the land on all sides, sprayed up veils of white against precipitous cliffs in an intimidating fashion.

He sat down on the hard bench seat behind him, thankful to have this vision of impending doom temporarily hidden by the side of the boat and wishing that the seabirds would cease their mournful, screeching reminders of his whereabouts. Delightful sojourns in the balmy warmth of Mediterranean islands had not prepared him for this inhospitable mound, situated off the west coast of Scotland and scrubbed perpetually by the cold Atlantic Ocean.

That his ignorance of the place was imminently to be corrected had not been of his own seeking. He was proceeding to Tora under duress, having failed to alter his father's conviction that he must go, and it had been a most unwelcome shock for him to face his father in such a mood of blind obstinacy. Generally, he had been spoiled for all of his twenty-eight years, compensation, undoubtedly, for the fact that he was the second male offspring, not the all important heir to the Strathcairn estate. He was, however, Uncle James's heir to Tora, as he and Aunt Elizabeth had no family. Hence the reason he had been landed with this assignment.

Unceremoniously summoned from Capri, he had initially been incredulous that his father actually expected him to comply with his uncle's request.

'What can I do? He needs a doctor, not me. I hardly know the man, for goodness' sake!'

'Precisely!' his father interjected. 'It's time you got to know him and faced up to your responsibilities.'

'Despite the fact that you spent one of the most miserable weeks of your life, incarcerated on the self-same island?' Alexander countered sarcastically.

'I'm not his beneficiary! You are, young man, and, as he's evidently confined to bed, he wants to see you.'

They were seated in Sir David's study at Strathcairn during this debate, and Alexander looked out disconsolately on to the rolling lawns which surrounded the mansion house at the centre of their vast family estate, ten miles from Dundee, over which his father presided as laird.

'But he's not at death's door, is he?' muttered Alexander crossly.

'I doubt he'd announce it in writing, even if he was,' retorted Sir David,with equal ill-humour. 'The old fool probably thinks he's immortal!'

Alexander might have reminded his father that the 'the old fool' was four years his junior, but he finally deduced, 'You're worried about him?'

'Of course – he's my brother after all, even if we've rarely seen eye to eye on anything, and particularly that damned island of his.'

'Perhaps, if you and mother hadn't painted such an awful picture of the place after your visit, I'd be more enthusiastic,' murmured Alexander, beginning to feel a measure of guilt and endeavouring to unload at least some of the blame. Ever since this excursion, when his father and mother had gone to Tora to attend his Aunt Elizabeth's funeral, his inheritance had been something of a standing joke in the family. Alexander had been a mere sixteen years old at the time, but he remembered the joyous clamour of their return. His mother had claimed that it would take her all of a week to thaw out and it had taken her a great deal longer to recover from the ordeal.

'Little wonder, poor Elizabeth did not see forty,' had been an oft repeated assertion of Lady McNair, which appeared to sum up her aversion to the place, while her husband had been prone to remind her that 'poor Elizabeth' had been responsible for his brother's insane obsession with Tora, as it had come to him through her family.

The experience, of course, had never been repeated, and Alexander had only been at home during one other visit by his uncle to Strathcairn, when he had been a guest at the wedding of his elder brother, Eric. At this juncture, Alexander had been a mere twenty-two years old, and in the throes of his first love for the junior bridesmaid. Consequently, he had not been greatly interested in his eccentric uncle, who was going to leave him a barren inhospitable blob of land, somewhere in the Atlantic.

Meanwhile, Sir David tried to correct the poor impression of the island which he and his wife had created. 'A funeral ... middle of winter ... no time to judge anything. In fact, I'd go with you on this occasion, but Eric's been feeling poorly again of late.'

Alexander merely nodded, resisting the urge to make a barbed comment about his elder brother, who now shared the running of the Strathcairn estate with his father. Their dislike of each other was a well-known phenomenon, which appeared to have its origins in the fact that while Eric was heir to the vast McNair fortune, Alexander had inherited all the good looks, health and capacity for enjoying life, which his brother had been denied.

'I wish you and he got on better,' said Sir David, shrewdly

interpreting his son's silence for restraint. 'There's a place for you on the estate, as well.'

Alexander smiled grimly. 'Under Eric's feet, Papa! No thanks.' His smile widened before he added wickedly, 'I might become besotted with Tora like Uncle James.'

His father snorted. 'You're too fond of the easy life! As soon as that place falls into your hands, you'll get rid of it, and a good job too.'

'I don't suppose Uncle James would appreciate that piece of *advice*,' said Alexander, goaded into sarcasm by his father's peremptory tone.

One of Sir David's glowering eyebrows twitched warningly. 'It's easy to aspire to be a paragon of honesty, Alexander, when one imagines there's a never-ending source of revenue at one's disposal. But there could be a yawning gulf between what you imagine and cold reality, if you choose to lose your inheritance – such as it is – through downright stupidity.'

'I just don't like the idea of deceiving him,' retorted Alexander angrily.

'It's not a question of deception,' Sir David barked at him. 'It's a question of common sense; that island will never be a profitable venture. How James has kept his head above water all these years, I'll never know.'

'Well, perhaps I'll find out during my visit,' he declared shortly, ending the discussion on a decidedly icy note.

Alexander started from his reveries on the bench seat, when he looked up to see a sheer cliff-face, which had materialized to tower dauntingly over the small steamer. Tora now lay a mere hundred yards away, but there was yet no sign of the harbour. The rim of his hat touched his collar as he gazed, fascinated, high into the sky to see the ragged summit of the land, which was being pounded by a swelling ocean of vibrant green, crusted with frothy white sprays that wet his face as he looked.

'It's a fine sight, is it not?'

Alexander turned, swallowing on his dry throat, as he realized that one of the two-man crew had been standing watching him – with evident amusement.

'Formidable,' he murmured unenthusiastically. To his amazement, he noticed then a figure, perched on a ledge near the top of the edifice. 'What's that fool trying to do – kill himself?'

'He's collectin' eggs,' the crewman called back over the roar of the waves and the clamour of the struggling engine. Approaching, he lowered his voice, 'It's not as dangerous as it looks. He'll know that cliff-face like his hand.'

He had a pleasant lilting quality to his voice and Alexander glanced in a measured fashion at this individual, whose knowledgeable calm was faintly irritating in the circumstances. His face – what could be seen of it beyond an unruly iron-grey beard – had a weathered strength of character about it, that was further enforced by the directness of his brown eyes.

'You're a native of the island, I presume?'

'Born and bred.'

'You'll know my uncle, then, the proprietor?'

'Everyone on Tora knows Mr McNair. And you're his nephew.'

Alexander smiled at his effortless familiarity. 'I wasn't aware my coming had been telegraphed.'

'Tora tongues are faster than the post.'

'You have me at a disadvantage then, Mr . . . ?'

'Graham. Neil Graham. Crofter, fisherman and on Thursdays, ferryman.'

As they shook hands, Alexander commented, 'Varied occupations.'

'Tora folk can turn a hand to anythin'. But you'll be findin' that out for yourself.' As he smiled suddenly, Alexander realized that he was probably no more than fifty – younger than he had initially thought. 'My, but you've had a braw day for the crossin', Mr McNair!' he exclaimed, glancing all round at the sky, which was now conjuring up patches of blue. 'That's Tora Point we've just passed,' he continued, waving his thick navy cap at the cliffs, which were now tapering down to a less intimidating height. 'You thought the swell was fierce today, I'll be bound, but you should see it in January! Standin' on the top you can get a fair wash with the spray.'

'Do you lose many boats in such conditions?'

'Before we got our harbour at Castlebay, there was hardly a year went by without a tragedy. But you'll be knowin' we've got your uncle to thank for that.'

As Alexander knew no such thing, he was glad when Graham began pointing with his cap once more. 'We're comin' into Castlebay now. Yonder's the harbour wall, and on the hill at the back you'll see Castle Tora.'

The bay was half-moon shaped, as if the ocean had taken a giant bite from the land, and Alexander was surprised to see stretches of incredibly white sand – all apparently deserted. From the plateau of the shore, undulating moorland rose over low rolling hills, and, directly overlooking the harbour, he could see his uncle's infamous castle. From the distance, it looked distinctly medieval and its grey colour reminded him of the daunting rock formations at Tora Point. Standing tall on a hill, it dwarfed the cluster of neat white buildings below that evidently made up the village of Castlebay, and its position – as if guarding the harbour against intruders – lent it an air of military grandeur. At one extremity was a square turret with battlements, while a lower circular turret marked the opposite side. There was a stark beauty to the scene, which surprised him, with the surrounding hills stained lighter by the fretful sun. Lonely crofts dotted the hillsides, and to the left, in the far distance, the great peak of Mount Tora towered over all, with a delicate lace crown of snow.

Alexander's stomach churned with unexpected excitement at the thought that one day this could all be his, and he quickly reminded himself of his father's strong wishes in the matter. The idea of duping his uncle into thinking that he would cherish his inheritance appealed even less now, however, with their meeting so imminent, and it occurred to him, as he glanced at Neil Graham, who was expertly manoeuvring the vessel into harbour, that he would also be deluding an unknown number of islanders – all of whom were dependent upon their proprietor's benevolence.

CHAPTER TWO

BY any standards, Alexander McNair was a striking-looking individual, long accustomed to drawing admiring glances, particularly from the opposite sex, and at over six feet, he might have stood out in a crowd through height alone. However, he had other attractions.

His hair was not merely dark, but had a definite blue-blackness that provided a startling contrast to the distinct grey of his eyes, which seemed to possess the chameleon-like quality of reflecting colours around him. His skin was generally tanned from his frequent excursions abroad and he smiled widely to display strong white teeth that were the particular envy of his brother, Eric, who saw such flashes of brilliance as annoying evidence of his younger brother's vanity.

In fact, Alexander's appearance gave him little satisfaction, as it needed no effort on his part and it was, perhaps, his careless disregard for his looks, which really irritated Eric, who instinctively resented qualities he could not buy. Intellectually, Alexander had also proved the superior, despite arduous efforts on Eric's part to set unassailable records at the private school they had both attended in Edinburgh, and Eric liked nothing better than reminding everyone that his younger brother had succeeded only in being expelled before he had completed the course. That Alexander had actively sought this expulsion, to avoid a final reckoning of achievements between him and his brother, would have been inexplicable to Eric, or his father, as neither could have understood that it had been infinitely more important for him to opt out of the unofficial competition, which had reigned for as long as he could remember.

Thus, Alexander took pride only in being everything that Eric was not: an idle spendthrift whose one apparent goal in life was to see the world before he was thirty. That he was only able to achieve this, courtesy of a continuing generous allowance from his father, was, nowadays, a constant bone of contention, but Alexander had lived so long with the deep-rooted conviction that second sons were little more than superfluous understudies in the ancestral scheme of things, that he yet felt no real guilt over this – just as he had never felt needed. Rather, he was a luxury his father could easily afford, even if Sir David did complain about the expense on occasion.

When Alexander disembarked on Tora, the quay at Castlebay was bustling with activity, as the fishing fleet had recently returned to harbour, and many of the boats were still being unloaded of their catches. Overhead, a multitude of seagulls screeched an unholy welcome to the feast of titbits coming their way and dozens of women were cloistered, chattering, around three enormous iron baths, their backs bent to the bloody task of gutting the accumulating mounds of fish. Others packed and sorted it, flounder with flounder, mackerel with mackerel, herring with herring. Young children played nearby while their mothers worked, and older youngsters performed allotted tasks – moving barrels, carrying buckets and sharpening blunted knives. Men transported heavy baskets, stacked with gutted fish to other prescribed areas – some for the island curers, some for the mainland and some for eating at islanders' tables that very night.

Neil Graham, although occupied with unloading his own cargo of mail and supplies, shouted, '*Soraidh*, Mr McNair,' and gave a saluting wave before Alexander climbed on to solid ground, to gaze wonderingly at the organized bustle of activity around him. Almost at once, however, he was aware that the pace of the work was slackening in response to his arrival. Women turned from the iron baths, covertly nudging their neighbours who did likewise; burdens were laid down while eyes were raised to linger upon him; even the children stopped their play to mutter and point.

Unable to comprehend a word of the hushed choir of Gaelic tongues which rose around him, Alexander smiled inanely in every direction, as he prayed for rescue. Some of the younger women, who wore brightly coloured polka-dot blouses and skirts or printed dresses, smiled back, but the matrons in their ranks, dressed uniformly in dark garments, remained tight-lipped. The men, too, were not so easily impressed. Some regarded him with open suspicion, while others looked with dour intensity, or faint amusement, much like Neil Graham.

Alexander flattened the collar of his heavy nap coat self-consciously, undid the buttons and removed his hat, as he endeavoured to assume a look of lofty indifference. In fact, his eyes were searching the quay for some means of conveyance out of there. He finally noticed a dogcart standing at the entrance to the quay and he had started to move towards it, even although it appeared to have no driver, when a voice hailed him from behind. Turning, he saw his uncle emerging, hale and hearty, from a group of fishermen.

They shook hands warmly. 'Alexander – good to see you, m'boy. Elsewhere, I don't think I'd have known you. You don't resemble your father one bit.' He seemed inordinately pleased by this quite accurate assessment. Alexander took after his mother's side; in particular, one great Uncle Henry, whose portrait hung in the gallery at Strathcairn, and whose womanizing exploits were as legend as the debts he had incurred.

'I think I was twenty-two when I saw you last.'

'Too long ago – and in rather different surroundings. You always managed to be absent, when I called in at Strathcairn,' he added with a wry smile. 'This must seem like another world to you.'

'Especially as I'm not conversant in the Gaelic.'

'Most of them can speak English when they want to.'

In that case, they were all listening, Alexander realized, and he lowered his voice to a whisper. 'We thought you were ill!'

'Oh that!' exclaimed his uncle, not at all embarrassed. 'I had to get you here somehow, didn't I? Never felt better in my life.'

That he had been thoroughly duped was now perfectly clear to Alexander, but with the whole island looking on, it hardly seemed time to advertise this fact. Instead he hissed urgently, 'Can we get out of here now, Uncle? I feel like an inmate at the zoo.'

'They don't see many like you here, dear boy. But come along! I've got the cart waiting.'

He promptly gave instructions for Alexander's luggage to be loaded on to the cart and they set off amidst a chorus of, '*Soraidh*, Mr McNair.'

The road up to Castle Tora was narrow, but surfaced, unlike many of the tracks over the island, as Alexander was later to discover. They therefore rattled along at a good pace through Castlebay village with its two shops, post office and small library among rows of neat little houses. From there on, the incline became steeper and the road more perilous, as the ground sloped away steeply on both sides, with only low stone dykes separating the dogcart from a nasty drop. The distinctive odours of the harbour gave way to the tangy aroma of peat, and James sniffed the air appreciatively.

'You'll have to get used to the smell of the peat in these parts. It keeps us warm and cooks all our food.'

'I expect there will be lots of things to get used to,' murmured Alexander, wondering how long he would be expected to stay, now that his uncle had staged a miraculous recovery.

As if sensing something of his thoughts, James said cheerfully, 'We sometimes get cut off from the mainland for weeks at a time, you know, when the weather turns foul.'

'I don't think you'll have to pray for storms to keep me here,

Uncle,' retorted Alexander lightly, 'not if you're honest with me.'

'Being honest didn't get you here, though, did it?' responded James with a tolerant smile. 'I've invited you all of six times at my last count and you've always had something more urgent to do.'

'*Touché*!' muttered Alexander, smiling along with him. 'But we'll need to send word to my father. He fears you're knocking at the pearly gates.'

'Trust David to imagine that I'd get there before him. He thinks he's immortal, you know. All that money he makes and keeps on making. He'll never spend a fraction of it, if he outlives Moses.'

'Ideas of immortality seem to run in the family,' observed Alexander with a laugh. 'And as for the money, I 'm helping him spend it. He doesn't approve, I'm afraid.'

'Naturally – he's a hoarder.'

Alexander laughed again, enjoying his uncle's banter and the way he spoke to him like an equal – unlike his father – who still persisted too often in treating him like a wayward infant. It occurred to him that he and his uncle might have a great deal more in common than he had imagined – both the 'redundant' sons of wealthy men – and that he had been foolish in accepting for so long the established image of James as the 'old imbecile' who resided on Tora.

His uncle was certainly not in his dotage. On the contrary, he was a remarkably young-looking fifty-year-old with only patches of white in his dark hair. He was a much finer featured man than his father; leaner too, and his clean-shaven skin was a healthy bronze from his outdoor activities. His blue eyes were a similar colour to his father's, but absent was the inscrutable glacial quality which frequently masked Sir David's thoughts. James appeared a more approachable individual, Alexander thought, although he did wonder whether his affability concealed more serious aspects to his personality. Certainly, his determined dedication to island life, apparently against strong advice to the contrary, paralleled his father's devotion to Strathcairn. But clearly their motivation was very different.

The horse had now slowed to a walking pace on the steep road, and Alexander began to wonder at its ability to make the climb, as it stood scarcely bigger than a pony, between eleven and twelve hands high.

'Are all the horses like this on the island?' he asked,

'I have a couple of big mares for riding, but for the real work we have to breed them like this. They're ideally suited to ploughing and carrying the peats.'

'Stronger than they look then?'

'Strong, sure-footed and hardy! We stable them nowadays, but they used to fend for themselves all the year round on whatever they could forage.'

'A hard life!'

'There's no mollycoddling around here, laddie!'

'Is that a warning?'

'Oh – I'll let you settle in first, before I get out the whip.' They both laughed, but Alexander again wondered uncomfortably what James had in mind for him and was very much afraid that he was going to have to disillusion him.

Castle Tora was no less impressive viewed from the flagstoned courtyard beneath its turrets and the scenic panorama below was splendid, with the sun now gifting the ocean with ribbons of silver light and the harbour filled with the boats of the small fleet. The land all around stretched away in gentle undulations of velvety moor and, unlike his mother, he saw in the absence of trees an ethereal kind of beauty, strangely dignified by the poverty of lush greenery which abounded on Strathcairn. Certainly, it was wild, uncivilized-looking country, but he was moved by the indomitable grandeur of it all in a way that he had never been touched by Strathcairn's more obvious attractions.

Suddenly, he was aware that his uncle was watching him and although he smiled enigmatically, it was as if James had read his thoughts.

'Wait until you see it in July with the gold of the broom and then in August when the heather's out in endless carpets of purple.'

Alexander was about to point out that this was only April and he had no intention of staying that long, but his uncle resumed, 'Do you notice the silence, too?'

In fact, the place was not silent: the horse snorted; a lone gull screeched overhead; and insects buzzed unseen in the grassland: yet, these noises only served to emphasize the rare quality of tranquillity that did, indeed, hang over the place like a transparent blanket, not of this world.

'Do you have any gardens to the rear of the castle,' Alexander asked, suddenly anxious to disturb the mesmerizing quality of the atmosphere, which was tugging strangely at his senses.

'I have a couple of acres under cultivation for food purposes, some outhouses and stables. When your aunt was alive, we had some flower-beds, but I've no time for the pampering she gave blooms to keep them alive in these parts.' He paused, waving one hand at his castle. 'Well – what do you think of it?'

'It's all very impressive!'

'Ah – here's Seorus Dhu!'

Alexander turned to see a peculiar-looking man, who had appeared around one side of the castle.

'What did you call him?' he enquired softly, as the man approached exhibiting a peculiar lopsided gait. He seemed to be galloping in an angular fashion towards them, every so often having to correct his navigation with a side-step or two, accompanied by a gaping smile. He was dressed like a tramp and over his mop of streaked grey hair, he wore an enormous checked bonnet, the skip of which shaded one ear. His vast grins displayed teeth like the bars of a wrecked gaol, and the odour from him reached Alexander's nostrils, before he did.

'His name's Seorus Dhu – in English, black George. He's not quite the full shilling, of course, and he used to make a pest of himself in the village, until I discovered he had a way with animals and gave him a job in the stables up here. He manages them all by himself and also keeps the castle supplied with peat.'

As Alexander braced himself for the introduction, his uncle muttered consolingly, 'He's as obedient as a lamb when he's reasonably sober, and his binges don't happen too often.'

The reek of whisky was certainly evident, as James said, 'Seorus, this is my nephew, young Mr McNair, who'll be staying at the castle for a time.'

Alexander was obliged to shake the grubby extended hand, as the man, head tilted to one side, gaped a wet smile at him without uttering a word.

'You're not overdoing it today, are you?' James queried, making a drinking motion with one hand, to which Seorus responded with a vigorous shake of his head.

'You can see to the horse and cart then and take Mr McNair's luggage upstairs. Flora will show you his room.'

Seorus set about his duties enthusiastically, as James and Alexander proceeded indoors.

Inside the arched entrance of the castle, Alexander was greeted by a vaulted square hallway, from which a broad stone stairway curved upwards to a high balcony, fronted by a mahogany balustrade. Several doors led off the hall and he was to learn later than the place was a maze of corridors, passages and narrow staircases. His perusal now, however, was interrupted when an extremely attractive young woman emerged from a door set in the recess of the main stair.

'Mhairi-Anne, come and meet Alexander!' exclaimed James, urging her towards them. Alexander might have kissed her hand, so pleased was he to see this unexpected vision, but she precluded all contact with a nodding demure smile.

'Very pleased to meet you,' she murmured.

'Likewise,' said Alexander, swiftly appraising a face that had little claim to classical beauty, yet was all the more fascinating because of its flaws. Her forehead was a trifle high; her nose rather too slim; her almond-shaped eyes widely set and her mouth, generous to a degree, but together these features housed in a conventional oval shape and complemented by thick corn-coloured hair, braided around her head, were a bewitching compilation. She had wonderful transluscent skin, too, he noticed, and the glimmering jade green of her eyes was remarkable.

'Mhairi-Anne teaches school on the island and she also attends to most of my paperwork,' James explained. 'She lodges here at the castle, as there's no accommodation attached to the school itself.'

Alexander nodded, his eyes continuing to linger appreciatively on the woman. The apparent quality of her high-necked cream blouse and long dark skirt had already told him that she could not be a servant. 'What attracted you here to teach, Miss er . . . ?'

'It's Mrs, actually, Mr McNair,' she corrected mildly, in a voice which was both musical and husky. 'Mrs Graham – and I'm a native of Tora.'

Another Graham, thought Alexander, noting this coincidence, as he endeavoured simultaneously to conceal his disappointment at her marital status.

James said, 'It's Mhairi-Anne and Alexander, surely. We don't need to stand on formality here.'

'Of course,' agreed Alexander, before forcing himself to add, 'I'll look forward to meeting your husband.'

James coughed warningly, but too late. 'Mhairi-Anne's a widow.'

Alexander was full of false regrets.

'It was a long time ago,' she murmured.

'You scarcely look old enough to be married, far less a widow.'

One finely arched eyebrow rose to acknowledge this compliment – but the gesture, accompanied by a simmering smile, amounted to subtle contempt at the blatancy of his interest.

Alexander grinned back at her, ironically stimulated by her evident failure to be impressed.

She turned her attention exclusively to James. 'Calum said to tell you that he's gone to Port nam Magan. He hopes to be back for dinner.'

James nodded, before briefly explaining to Alexander that Calum was his overseer, who also resided at the castle. 'Did you manage to make sense of those stock figures?' he asked of Mhairi-Anne.

'We didn't lose half as many as last winter.'

'Good!' He turned to Alexander. 'We take a spring and pre-winter count of all the animals, so that we can keep track of losses and gains and work out the appropriate *soum* for each crofter.'

'What's the *soum*?'

'The number of animals a crofter can send to the common pastures beneath Mount Tora, so that the arable land around the villages can be cultivated without fear of the crops being eaten.'

'How large is the island?'

'About ten miles long by six at its widest point. With a population of around three hundred and each family having an average of twenty to twenty-five animals, we need every acre. The land will only support so many animals and the crofters sell their excess to pay rent and buy essential items, once the *soum* has been worked out.'

'If you'll excuse me James. . . .'

'Sorry Mhairi-Anne – we're keeping you.'

'I must let Flora know that Alexander has arrived and I have some corrections to do for school. Perhaps, you'd like some tea?' she suggested, glancing at Alexander.

'Tell Flora to bring it up to Alexander's room,' said James. 'Flora's my housekeeper,' he explained, as Mhairi-Anne moved off, the folds of her skirt rustling enticingly in Alexander's ears.

Over their tea, Alexander learned much more about Mhairi-Anne, as initially his uncle seemed only too willing to explain her background and the fact that she had been very much like a daughter to his late wife. She was twenty-seven and not a qualified teacher, according to James, but more than adequately equipped to teach the elementary schooling required on the island. Born the only child of crofters, her intelligence had first been spotted by Elizabeth, who had taken a keen interest in the pupils in the island school, which she had started. Subsequently, Elizabeth had persuaded Mhairi-Anne's parents that their clever daughter ought to continue her education on the mainland, after she had reached twelve years of age – an expense which the McNairs had met personally, due to their faith in the girl, and their long-term hope that she might ultimately teach on Tora. This mainland education, however, had been terminated when Mhairi-Anne had reached eighteen, as her mother had then died and her father had insisted upon her return to work on their croft.

'He was a dreadful boozer – her father,' said James reflectively. 'Elizabeth would have been heart-broken, if she'd still been alive when Mhairi-Anne went back there to work for him, but he was out to make trouble for me with the other islanders and she decided she could take no more "charity", as she had come to see it.'

The arrangement had not lasted, however. Mhairi-Anne had subsequently married to escape her father's tyranny, James suspected, and sometime after her marriage, her father had died of exposure, after lying out overnight on the moors, in a drunken stupor.

She had come to live at Castle Tora shortly after her husband, too, had died in a fishing accident at sea, and when the position of teacher in the island school had become vacant.

'She's certainly had more than a fair share of tragedy in her life,' observed Alexander. 'I take it she married an islander?'

James nodded. 'Neil Graham.'

'Is she related to the ferryman?' Alexander queried.

'Her husband was his eldest son.'

Alexander immediately thought it rather odd that during their conversation the precocious islander had failed to mention that his own daughter-in-law resided at the castle, and he said as much to James.

'Oh – Neil's a fine man in many ways, but he gets ideas into his head and there's no changing them.'

Alexander frowned at his uncle's sudden evasiveness, but was not allowed to pursue the point, as James rose abruptly from their tea. 'Come on! I'll give you a tour of the castle. Now I've managed to get you here, I don't want you getting lost before the day is out.'

Smiling, Alexander rose to follow his uncle's lead without further comment, but his interest in the island's teacher had only been further stimulated by the vague notion that James was hiding something.

CHAPTER THREE

ALEXANDER sent a note to his father the day after his arrival, briefly reassuring him that James was not about to depart for the hereafter and on Sunday morning, three days into his visit, he decided to write a letter, explaining that he intended to prolong his stay, in order to learn more about his inheritance.

James had now made it clear that he wanted him to remain indefinitely, as he seemed to believe that he would, in due course, fall under the spell of Tora, as he himself had done when he had first visited the island during his engagement to Aunt Elizabeth, many years before. In these circumstances, Alexander might well have considered it expedient to make a swift departure. Although he liked the place more than he could ever have anticipated, he had no wish to become *enchanted*, certain as this was to incur serious conflict with his father, and, equally so, the more he got to know James and the island, the less he relished the prospect of knowingly deceiving him. However, his interest in Mhairi-Anne Graham precluded any notion of a speedy return to the mainland, to avoid courting trouble. Over the past three days, he had decided that she was the most alluring creature he had ever met and he, consequently, did not seriously contemplate throwing away his opportunity to know her better.

He began his letter with the usual pleasantries, before rapidly explaining his intentions. The brevity of the epistle at this point seemed to invite unwanted curiosity, however, and he wrote on:

Your brother has not been as lonely in his castle, as we all thought. The island's schoolteacher, Mrs Graham, resides on the premises, as well as his overseer, Calum MacRitchie, who returned to the island some five years ago, with money to invest. We were wondering how Uncle James had managed to keep his head above water. I believe that Calum has been his life-raft. Actually, he is a native of Tora, who left in his youth to seek his fortune in Nova Scotia. This he did, but he never lost the yearning to return to his roots.

When I met him at dinner on the evening of my arrival he had just returned from an inspection trip to Port nam Magan, where there is a small natural harbour. It is proposed to build a pier on this site, in order to create an alternative harbour on the east coast of the island. Frequently, during winter storms, boats caught out are unable to round Tora Point and Port nam Magan has already been a life-saving shelter. The process of beaching boats there on a dark stormy night, however, is apparently a hazardous business, so that a pier seems like a sensible idea. Fortunately, Calum is again backing Uncle James in this philanthropic venture.

Having achieved all of two pages, he felt that he had probably assuaged his father's appetite for detail and, satisfied, he rose, stretching, as he wandered to the open window of his bedroom. It was a mild sunny morning and the vibrant smell of the peat instantly assailed his nostrils. From the church, which clung to the side of the small valley beyond the rear of the castle, the strains of Gaelic voices raised to psalm-singing carried on the light breeze and he leaned out of the casement to listen to this haunting sound. As he looked down, however, he saw Mhairi-Anne seated directly below on the stone dyke, her back to him and her attention focused on sketching the view before her. His interest in the psalm-singing was immediately forgotten, as he promptly careered out of his chamber, anxious to take advantage of this unexpected opportunity to see her alone. She glanced up as he approached, her expression startled, but she swiftly composed herself.

'I did not know drawing was another of your accomplishments,' he said, as he glanced over her shoulder at a sketch of the harbour below, which was being skilfully executed in charcoal.

'It's merely a hobby,' she responded dismissively.

'I thought you'd gone to church with the others,' he said, seating himself on the dyke, so that his back faced the scene she was sketching.

'I stopped that practice some years ago. Didn't James expect you to put in an appearance?'

Alexander shrugged. 'I did not relish the prospect of mouthing Gaelic hymns, while everyone on the island took a closer look at me. Perhaps, once I am less of a side-show.'

'That would please James.'

'The singing is oddly appealing,' he said, as the ethereal sound continued to drift over the moorland.

'It appears to have a spiritual quality in the open air,' she agreed. 'Inside the church, it sounds more earthly.'

'Why did you stop going?' he asked, as she continued to add shading to her drawing.

She shrugged. 'Generally, I am at odds with the ritual dogma of the church on Tora.' She looked up, a smile hovering on her lips. 'I should tell you that you're presently seated beside a sinner in the act of sinning.'

'Tell me more,' he murmured, holding her eyes for a brief moment, before she focused her attention once more on her sketch and added, 'I should not be sketching. All work and all pleasure are strictly forbidden on Sundays.'

'I'm disappointed. For a moment, I thought you had some dark secret.'

She looked up sharply, a fleeting tension in her expression. 'I have, but it would not be a secret, if I told you.'

'Now I'm really intrigued.'

She gazed at the handsome face and openly flirtatious smile for several seconds before she said, 'I think I should give you some friendly advice, Alexander.'

'Please do.'

'You would be wise to direct your charms elsewhere.'

He laughed. 'I'm gratified to know you're not immune to them.'

'But you are immune to advice, I see.'

'My father says I'm incorrigible.'

'I hope not.'

'I think I'm half in love with you already.'

Her mouth tightened and she made no response, as she very deliberately began to add sweeping lines to her drawing with an intensity of concentration that invited him to leave.

He was not to be dismissed so easily, however, and for a time he sat contentedly watching the sun glinting on her hair; admiring the sureness of her slim hand on the paper, and the grace of her neck and shoulders as she bent over her task. Another psalm rose hauntingly over the hills, before he murmured, as if to himself, 'I have been more than surprised by the appeal of this place.'

She glanced up. 'We had gathered you were not eager to come.'

'James told me my excuses had worn a trifle thin,' he responded, but not wishing to begin a discussion about his inheritance, he abruptly altered course. 'I met your father-in-law the other day on the ferry. Do you see much of him these days?'

'Did he mention me?' she countered, staring intently at the harbour scene.

'No – actually I thought it rather odd that he didn't, when I found out you were related.'

Carefully she added another dimension to her sketch, before she turned to him. 'I suppose you should know that he blames me for his son's death. Nowadays, he pretends I don't exist.'

'How can he possibly justify such an attitude? I believe your husband drowned at sea.'

'He fell overboard during a storm.'

'How can he attribute that to you?'

'You will find that I am accused of many things on Tora.'

'You say that as if you are unpopular.'

'I am.' His puzzled expression prompted her to add, 'I have risen above my station in life.'

'Yet you teach their children – well – by all accounts.'

'If it was up to the islanders, I would not occupy that position. There was much trouble when I took over initially. For a time I was a teacher without pupils, but your uncle made it a condition of tenancy that the children attend.'

Alexander was intrigued and incredulous, but he was prevented from enquiring further into this extraordinary phenomenon, when they heard the voices of Calum and James, who were approaching on the path. Church was evidently over.

'Getting some fresh air, Alexander!' James remarked. 'Did you write to your father?'

'Yes – a signature will finish it. How was church? I was rather impressed by the singing.'

'Everyone was in good voice this morning. We have finally reached the necessary sum to erect a commemorative statue of Elizabeth in the school forecourt.'

'The idea is to ensure that nobody ever forgets your aunt, Alexander,' said Mhairi-Anne. 'As if we would!' She suddenly stood up, her sketch under her arm. 'I think I'll go in. It's getting chilly.'

As she walked off, James responded to the puzzled frown on Alexander's face. 'Mhairi-Anne believes that Elizabeth would not have approved of this venture and that the money would be better spent on refurbishing the school itself.'

'She has a point,' said Calum.

'Don't you start,' responded James, clapping Calum good-naturedly on the back, as they all went in to lunch. 'You worry about getting our new harbour underway!'

Calum MacRitchie was more than ten years older than James, but still a vigorous man, who was now totally devoted to spending the remaining years of his life working for the good of his native island and its people. With wiry snow-white hair, a frizzy beard of a similar colour, twinkling blue eyes and portly figure, he might have fulfilled a child's notion of Santa Claus, and his philanthropic interest in Tora was certainly in keeping with this image. With no family on whom to bestow the small fortune he had made in Nova Scotia, he had returned to the island for the purpose of spending his accumulated wealth on his native soil, before he died, with no expectation of any return, except accommodation at the castle, and some say in how his money was spent. At first, James could not believe his luck and expected a hidden agenda. But there was none. He and Calum had developed a close partnership over the years, based on mutual liking and respect, and James now greatly appreciated the older man's advice, born of his vast experience in working the land during his pioneering days in Nova Scotia.

Over lunch, Calum amused them all with more amazing tales of his years in foreign parts and Alexander was again impressed by his ability to make comedy out of situations which would have routed the strongest of men. He had taken an instant liking to Calum on his first evening in the castle and this was developing into unstinting admiration, the more he knew of him. To Alexander, who had been brought up in an environment structured by mercenary concerns, social dogma and rules, an individual, who appeared to pay little heed to such, was a novel and refreshing creature. Calum made him feel ashamed, when he thought about his discussion with his father, prior to coming to Tora, and distinctly uncomfortable, when he considered what his intentions towards his inheritance were supposed to be.

Over their meal, it was decided that Calum would take Alexander on a tour of Tora the following day, to see some of the sights and meet some of the locals, while James would be embroiled in his monthly council meeting. This group consisted of ten elected islanders, who represented specific interests and allowed for debate of grievances, suggestions and questions. In effect, it gave the islanders a measure of democracy and Alexander was not surprised to learn that the idea had been promoted by Calum.

After lunch, with James and Calum poring over drawings related to the Port nam Magan harbour project, Alexander decided to take a walk and post his letter to his father. Mhairi-Anne had been decidedly quiet during the meal and she had vanished without saying how she intended to spend her time. He was thinking about her as he left the castle and it was almost as if his mind had conjured her up, when he saw her disappearing over the brow of an adjacent hill.

His letter was forgotten as, impulsively, he decided to follow her. When he reached the summit, however, he was panting and annoyed to find her nowhere in sight. He lurched down the slope, cursing as he went. Then he spotted her again, following a narrow pass between two smaller hills to his right. He proceeded on to a stony track that dipped sharply and twisted between a series of great boulders, which opened spectacularly, like curtains, on to a magic expanse of shore. A long strip of creamy white sand gave way to rocks and the blue of the ocean, white-capped with rolling waves.

The area was utterly deserted except for the lone figure of Mhairi-Anne, traversing the sand, a large basket over one arm. He called to her, but a strong wind swept his voice away like leaves, so that he was almost upon her when she turned and saw him.

'What are you doing here?' she demanded, but an amused smile played provocatively with her lips.

'Following you, of course. What are you up to?'

'Come and see.'

As they proceeded onto the rocks, she warned, 'Take care! They're slippery. James would never forgive me if you ended up breaking a leg, after all the trouble he had getting you here.'

'Any other woman I know would be expecting me to carry her,' he retorted, admiring the speed and agility with which she negotiated the jagged surfaces, despite the encumbrance of her long skirt. 'I see you've had plenty of practice at this.'

She leapt up on to a high rock ahead of him. 'Let me know if you need a hand,' she retorted cheekily.

'Now would be as good a time as any!' He held his hand up to her, but a glance at his playful face sent her scurrying over the rocks again without him.

He followed immediately, his laugh catching in the wind.

She finally came to a halt at a circular pool in the rocks, with water a couple of feet deep, and by the time he arrived beside her she had laid down her basket, removed her shoes and was wading towards her objective – a small submerged cage, which contained a number of very large and lively crabs.

'Perhaps, you can open the other basket,' she suggested, as she waded back clutching her prize.

He had a brief glimpse of shapely bare limbs, before she dropped her skirt and fell to her knees to begin transferring a number of crabs from the cage to her open basket, gripping the creatures skilfully by their hard shells, so that their menacing claws were rendered ineffective.

'That will be enough, I think. If you fasten the lid, I'll return these to the pool.'

Expecting another glimpse of naked limbs, he was disappointed when she simply tossed the container back into the middle of the water, where it promptly submerged in a rush of bubbles.

'Is this one of your regular jobs?' he asked, as she sat down with her back to him to put on her shoes again.

'John put them there to keep them fresh, as there was a large catch of crabs on Friday.' John, Alexander now knew, was Flora's husband, who did heavier jobs around the castle. 'He was supposed to retrieve some of them yesterday, but with his extra work, he forgot.'

'Extra work?' echoed Alexander, as they set off back over the rocks, the basket now in his hands.

'On Saturday, the islanders do everything for Sunday as well.

Meals are made ready for serving, peats carried in adjacent to the fires and so on. Flora intended to make crab soup last night, but discovered too late that the crabs were missing.'

'So you, being a sinner, volunteered to fetch them!'

'And make the soup! Flora and John are not as dogmatic as many on the island, but they do as little as possible on the Sabbath. They will serve the meals, as usual, of course, but most of the clearing up will be left until tomorrow.'

'So you will be responsible for this delicacy at dinner this evening?'

'Don't worry! I dare say Flora's conscience will stretch to keeping me right.'

'I will relish every drop,' he assured her, mischievously licking his lips in anticipation.

She cast him an admonishing glance. 'Your father is right. You are incorrigible!'

'A self-confessed sinner – like you,' he retorted.

'That will not endear you to the islanders. Every day, people are kneeling to pray before their work begins and in the evenings there are Bible readings in almost every house. They are also very superstitious in their beliefs and would not break their daily routine for anything.'

'You speak as if you are not a native yourself.'

'I was never comfortable with the ritual of it all.'

'Perhaps this is another reason you are not popular?'

She shrugged. 'I am resigned to being a black sheep.'

'They seem to have held Aunt Elizabeth in high esteem.'

'The highest! She was indeed a wonderful woman. I was very fond of her.'

'But you disapprove of this statue business.'

'James told you?'

He nodded. 'Whose idea was it?'

'I believe my father-in-law had a hand in it and the Reverend Morrison, of course.'

They had now reached the sand and she stopped to gaze out

at the ocean and sky, across which great white clouds were scudding in intricate moving patterns. 'The tide's turning,' she murmured thoughtfully, as Alexander studied the sudden wistfulness of her expression.

'Why do you stay here?' he asked impulsively

'Where I'm not wanted?' She smiled and shrugged. 'Calum came back after years away. It's hard to explain. This island has a way of keeping its souls.' She walked on again, taking the stony track back to the castle.

James and Calum were having their customary Sunday afternoon smoke of their pipes at the castle door, when they appeared together over the brow of the hill.

'I thought he was goin' to post a letter,' said Calum, his blue eyes narrowing as he watched their progress over the slope.

'That's what he said.'

Calum turned and glanced at him meaningfully.

'Why are you looking at me like that?'

'There's too much secrecy around here, James. That's what I'm thinkin'.'

'You worry too much! No wonder your hair's so white.'

'Aye – an' you'll be tellin' me next that they don't make a grand-lookin' couple.'

'He's only a laddie, Calum!'

Calum snorted disparagingly. 'That's auld age talkin'! You'd been married three years to Elizabeth, at his age, and he's all of six months older than her. If he's a laddie, she's nowt but a lass – an' you're an auld goat goin' blind, if you can't see what's happenin' in front of your face!'

CHAPTER FOUR

THE following morning, Alexander and James breakfasted alone, Mhairi-Anne having already departed for the schoolhouse and Calum, an habitual dawn-riser, was inspecting a cow which, according to Seorus Dhu, was about to calf.

Conversation centred initially on what Alexander might expect to see inside a 'black house' – the term given to a typical croft dwelling.

'We started calling them 'black houses', when 'white houses' – built from stone and lime, with felt or slated roofs – began to be erected in the island villages,' James explained. 'You'll probably be shocked initially. They're primitive dwellings, by any standards.'

'Was Mhairi-Anne born in one of these black houses?'

'Yes, and Calum, of course.' He paused before continuing tentatively, 'About Mhairi-Anne . . . I . . . er. . . .'

Alexander glanced up from his delicious kippers to see his uncle fidgeting uncomfortably.

'I . . . see you're rather . . . enamoured with her,' James finally blurted out.

'You could say that,' responded Alexander, totally unabashed.

'Don't be getting too fond of her, will you? You know nothing could come of it with your background and your father would strongly disapprove, of course.' He manufactured a jerky laugh. 'I'd much rather you fell in love with Tora.'

'You're the last person I expected to hear issuing such advice,

Uncle. You've made a lifetime's habit of disagreeing with my father.'

James laughed again at this, but he was clearly rattled, while Alexander was becoming increasingly intrigued.

'I'm not trying to dictate to you, like your father would. You're young, impressionable . . . it's easy to see why you're taken with her, but—'

'You're behaving like some distraught father, struggling to impart a lecture on the facts of life, Uncle,' Alexander interjected mockingly. 'What are you trying to say exactly?'

'Just that I want you to enjoy your time here, without complications.'

'I hardly know the woman, for heaven's sake. Seems to me this is all rather premature. It's not as if I'm planning to elope with her on the next ferry.'

'No, but she's not to be taken lightly either.'

'An affair – I should be so lucky!'

James snorted in annoyance. 'I can see you're not taking any of this seriously.'

'On the contrary, I'm curious to know why you're getting so worked up.'

'I've told you! I don't want complications. Your visit here is very important to me, Alexander, and to the future of this island.'

Alexander looked down at his plate, wondering if this was the moment for him to be honest, but his uncle went on, 'Unfortunately, tragedy has dogged the footsteps of men who have become attached to her.'

'Now you sound like a superstitious islander,' said Alexander, stabbing at his food. 'She tells me she's unpopular. No wonder, if you encourage thinking like this.'

'It's not a question of encouraging it. People talk, superstition is part of life in these parts and this goes back a long way.'

'What do you mean?'

'There was her father's death, of course, but her name was initially linked with a young lad – they were both about sixteen,

I think, at the time. Mhairi-Anne was home on holiday from school, when the boy went egg-collecting and fell off the cliffs at Tora Point.'

'I saw a man on the cliffs the other day. It looked like a thoroughly dangerous occupation.'

'Of course – and the association with Mhairi-Anne meant little back then, but with the later tragedies, she's come to be regarded as a kind of bad luck symbol. Another man died along with her husband, you know.'

'Another man?'

'He was trying to save Neil and drowned as well.'

'But no rational person could blame her for any of these deaths, Uncle. It's all down to medieval thinking and I'm afraid if your intention was to discourage me, this conversation has had precisely the opposite effect. I think that she needs all the friends she can get.'

'Friends – yes!' retorted James.

At that moment, the door to the breakfast-room opened and Calum came in. James sat back in his chair, as if relieved at this interruption.

'How's the cow?' he asked.

'Doing fine she is, although it will be a few hours' hard labour yet. You might get John to keep an eye on her and Seorus Dhu. He's lookin' as peaky as the cow this mornin'.'

James nodded and Calum turned to Alexander. 'Well, are you ready for the grand tour?'

Alexander stood up. 'Can't wait!'

They were just about to leave in the dogcart, when Neil Graham approached the castle on foot and Calum stopped to have a word with him

'You'll be pleased with the news at the council meetin' today, Neil. We're goin' ahead with the pier at Port nam Magan.'

'That's good to know on a Monday mornin',' responded Graham cheerfully. 'And how are you enjoyin' your visit, Mr McNair?'

'It's all very interesting,' Alexander answered, before succumbing to a reckless impulse. 'I've been pleased to meet your daughter-in-law.'

His reaction might have been deemed comical, had it not been so weird. The smile dropped from his face, like a discarded skin, and he gazed blankly at Alexander, without uttering a word, as if he had suddenly lost consciousness.

'We'll need to be off, Neil,' Calum muttered, flicking the reins so sharply, the horse pawed the ground.

Graham came to life again. 'Aye! I'll be seein' you.'

'You had to do that, I suppose,' said Calum as the horse trotted off.

'The man's obviously deranged,' responded Alexander disparagingly.

'Neil Graham's as sane as you or me, and you shouldn't go meddlin' in things you don't understand.'

'Can you explain why he blames Mhairi-Anne for his son's death?'

Calum shrugged. 'I believe there was a row before young Neil went out on his boat that night.'

'Everyone has rows! There must be more to it than that.'

'Aye – feelings – gossip and human nature! Mhairi-Anne tends to have a powerful effect on folk.'

'It's as if they think she's some kind of witch, from what I can gather.'

'I dare say the more fanciful ones would have you believe she can fly.'

'It's all so unfair! That fellow Graham ought to be horse-whipped for his attitude.'

'I'd like to see the man that would try it.' He glanced at Alexander's taut face. 'Forget him, laddie! And cool down whatever it is you've got burnin' inside you for Mhairi-Anne.'

Alexander smiled at this. 'Now, you sound like Uncle James.'

'He's spoken to you then?'

'This morning.'

'Well, you've been warned!'

Alexander fell silent then. While he was aware that his father would disapprove of such a relationship on the grounds of class alone, he could not believe that he was already facing opposition here. It all seemed out of character and unnecessary, considering that there was absolutely nothing between them, in any case. Calum and James had obviously noted his interest, but so what? Clearly, they did not know him very well. Forbidden fruit had always tasted sweeter to him.

They visited several black houses that day and initially Alexander was appalled at the living conditions. Even from the outside, they were strange-looking structures. About forty-five feet in length, they were low and rectangular in shape, but had rounded corners. The thick walls and lack of windows gave them the appearance of tiny fortresses, and although the thatched roofs rustled and creaked in the wind, they too were apparently robust. The doors were made in two sections – the top part often open to allow light in and smoke out. With his height, Alexander had to stoop low on entering, but he was amazed at their capacity. All of the inmates of the croft, including the animals, had shelter here, and their design had apparently evolved over the years as that best suited to standing up against the formidable storms that tore over the island. Thatch was easily repaired, he was told, if a section was lost.

Inside, every inch of floor space was filled with furnishings of a strictly practical nature: kists for holding clothes, or meal; a table and chairs made with straw and hide; low three-legged stools, logs and even large stones provided extra seating; and box-beds called *crubs*, were built into the walls to form partitioned sleeping areas with some privacy and separation of male and female children. The byre was divided from the domestic quarters by another partition created by the chimney.

The main cooking utensil was a black iron, three-legged pot with a removable handle, which fitted smaller pots and a griddle. Agricultural implements, fishing gear, wash tubs and spinning wheels were also evident and on every croft he found people hard at work – weaving, digging peats, mending nets, baking, attending animals – an endless array of tasks, all seemingly undertaken with an enthusiasm he could only admire. Indeed, his initial shock at the way these people lived shortly gave way to appreciation of how well they survived and how skilful they were.

Calum told him that the women had a heavier share of the work and quoted an old Gaelic proverb that highlighted this: *Is aoibhneas gach tigh, teine more is deagh bheann* – The cause of joy in every house is a big fire and a capable wife. Thinking of Mhairi-Anne in this context, he thought he could understand better why she had become anathema to her fellow islanders and why, perhaps, she and her husband had not prospered. The elegance of her appearance was totally at odds with the sturdiness of the women he saw that day. She simply did not fit in, he concluded.

Calum also quoted another Gaelic proverb – his favourite, he said: *An rud a thig leis a' gaoith, falbhaidh e leis an uisg* – What comes on the wind, the floods will sweep away.

'I'm not sure what it implies,' Alexander confessed.

'That life – love – we mortals, are transitory, lad. Time and nature are relentless and we are only flotsam on the wind.'

'You sound like a poet, Calum.'

'Och, but it sums it all up, doesn't it?'

The fishing fleet was returning to the harbour when they came into Castlebay village, and as Calum indicated that he intended to take care of some business with a certain fisherman, Alexander decided to post his father's letter, which he still had in the pocket of his tweed jacket.

'I'll pick you up in the village when I'm through,' Calum promised. 'I won't be long,'

In the post office, Alexander came face to face with Mistress Effie MacCulloch, the central pole in the gossip network on Tora. Her ample frame included a bosom, which shook like two enormous dumplings as she spoke, a diversion which caused

Alexander constant problems in maintaining eye contact. Her technique included putting words in her victims' mouths.

'You'll be enjoying your stay, Mr McNair?'

'You'll find life here rather different, Mr McNair?'

'Your family has an estate near Dundee, I hear?'

'You'll not have met Mr MacRitchie before?'

'Nor Mrs Graham?'

Alexander immediately noticed a longer pause here appeared to invite more than a monosyllabic response and he willingly obliged. 'A most charming, intelligent woman. But I expect you all realize how fortunate you are to have her teaching the children.'

Effie emitted a nasal sound, her hybrid of 'Yes' and 'No'.

Alexander assumed a puzzled expression before elaborating, 'She's had a tragic life, I believe, but I suppose that the islanders all rally round in such circumstances.'

'Mrs Graham's the independent type! Needs no help from anybody!' The words exploded from Effie like volleys of bullets, squeezed from a rusty gun.

'Oh, I daresay she would be choosy about her friends,' countered Alexander, deriving malicious delight from the woman's obvious discomfiture.

Her cold eyes steadied on his face and her bosom heaved, as she said slowly, 'I saw her taking a stroll on the beach yesterday with one of her friends. Couldn't quite make out who it was, but a man, as you might expect.'

Alexander smiled venomously. 'I trust you did not get sand in your eyes Mistress MacCulloch. There was quite a gale blowing, if I remember correctly.' He then promptly wished her a good day and made for the door.

Outside he stood fuming silently at the thought of this woman spreading further rumours about Mhairi-Anne all over the island. He should have flattered the old witch, he concluded angrily.

'Mr McNair . . . hello!'

He turned, startled by a quiet cultured voice behind him, to see a young woman of obvious breeding standing at the door of the small library. She wore a dark-green cloak and matching hat, which sat pertly on the front of her head while her hair was arranged in gleaming coils, the style of which alone would have told him she was not a Torean woman. And the heart-shaped face with its enormous brown eyes looked vaguely familiar.

'You don't remember me?' she murmured, obviously embarrassed.

'I'm sorry . . .'

'My name's Victoria Liversidge. We met briefly at a function in Perth.'

'Of course!' he exclaimed, the name instantly triggering a series of recollections. Although his memory of their meeting remained dim, he vividly recalled details of a case which had hit the headlines some time back. Widower, Jeremy Liversidge, a Perth businessman, had shot himself through the head, after a business speculation had left him penniless. In the papers, there had been much talk about his only daughter, 18-year-old Victoria, who had vanished immediately after his funeral. The tragedy had actually caused a debate between his parents over breakfast one morning, as they knew the man from a number of social events. Sir David had declared that Liversidge had been a damned fool, risking all his capital in such a venture, while his mother had insisted that he was a charming individual and that her husband was a 'callous brute' saying such a thing, in the wake of the man's death and his daughter's disappearance.

Alexander's face evidently betrayed him.

'You know about my father . . .' she murmured, her embarrassment now acute.

'I read of it,' he admitted. 'I'm sorry – I can see I have upset you.'

She raised a glimmer of a smile. 'On the contrary, I upset myself by imagining that people will soon forget such a scandal. I should be prepared to deal with it by now.'

'How do you come to be on Tora?'

'My father and your uncle became friendly through business dealings over the years. We had visited him here on Tora on several occasions before he . . . died. Your uncle could not attend the funeral, but he sent a letter inviting me to stay. I was in such a dreadful turmoil and I remembered how peaceful and isolated it was here. So I arrived on his doorstep.'

'But you're not staying at the castle now.'

'No – I've been here all of six months. Your uncle was kind enough to accommodate me for several weeks, until I recovered, but I could not go on living there on his charity. Fortunately, the library had just been completed and a librarian was needed. I volunteered for the position. There are two rooms attached to the back of the building, which suit me admirably. I am happy to have a little independence.'

'Do you have no family on the mainland?'

'None who is eager to share the burden of my renown.'

It struck Alexander that this island would destine her to lonely spinsterhood, when she could yet be no more than nineteen. She was hardly the stuff of a crofter's wife. Apart from the differences in class, she looked fragile in every sense.

'You will be glad of Mhairi-Anne's company on occasions, I suppose,' he said, breaking the growing silence between them.

'Indeed! She visits me often. We share a love of reading and, of course, she is such a talented painter.'

'I knew she sketched, but I have not seen any of her finished work.'

'I have three of her paintings in the library, if you care to look.'

'But weren't you leaving?'

'It's no trouble. Come – they are worth seeing.'

The paintings, all watercolours, were hung on the end wall of the building, beyond the rows of stacked bookshelves. The first was a view from Tora Point on a stormy day, with the waves rising dramatically over a beleaguered vessel. He was impressed by the way she had managed to capture the violence of the ocean and the vivid quality of the colours. In the second, a view of the castle, she had managed to convey the rugged grandeur of the thick stone walls and the austere beauty of the moorland. The third painting was a portrait of his uncle, or a younger version of him, he thought. The likeness was evident, but he felt that she had flattered him.

'I'm amazed,' he said, on finishing his perusal. 'She said her sketching was merely a hobby, but I believe these would sell on the mainland.'

'She is far too modest about her work, Indeed, she refused for a time to allow me to display these and insisted they be placed on the back wall, instead of at the entrance, when she finally agreed.'

'Perhaps, she thought that the islanders would not appreciate her talent.'

Victoria's face clouded. 'I do not really understand the attitude that prevails here. As an outsider, I am not privy to the usual gossip, and, of course, it is known that we are friends.'

They returned to the library entrance.

'I must go. Calum will be wondering where I've vanished. I expect I will see you soon at the castle.'

'Tonight, in fact. I received a message this morning, inviting me to dine.'

When he emerged into the street, Calum was already there, waiting in the dogcart.

'So you've been in Miss Victoria's safekeepin'! I was beginnin' to think the widow MacIver had grabbed you in the passing.'

'Who is the widow MacIver?' he enquired, as he hoisted himself on to the seat.

'A powerful sturdy woman with an urgent fire in her belly and no steady man to douse it.' He shook his head, chuckling softly as he did so. 'There's been many a fine man laid low by her.'

'A tart on Tora! You're joking, of course.'

'Not a tart – no – not in this Godfearin' haven, and Mrs

MacIver a regular churchgoer too. But she is one of a few generous widows in these parts, that a man need never be goin' to the mainland.'

Alexander laughed raucously, as they rattled on their way, and it was some time before he commented, 'Uncle James might have warned me that Victoria Liversidge was on the island.'

'He wanted to surprise you at dinner tonight. She said that she knew you.'

When they arrived at the castle, they noticed another vehicle at the entrance and Calum frowned. 'That's Dr Campbell's horse. Someone must be ill.'

They hurried inside, leaving the dogcart by the entrance, as Seorus Dhu was nowhere in sight. Indoors, they discovered that he was the patient, but John was rather vague about his ailment.

'I found him by the cow and her fine wee calf, staring into space, as if he had seen a ghost.'

'He'll have had too much whisky,' said Calum.

'But he's hardly had a tipple today, Mr MacRitchie. His bottle was there, still near full, in his pocket.'

Their speculations were terminated, when James and Dr Campbell appeared.

'How is the old rascal?' asked Calum. 'I thought he was lookin' a bit off colour this mornin'.'

'Seorus will probably outlive all of us,' said the doctor cheerfully, 'except you, young man!' He glanced from Alexander to James. 'No need to tell me who this is, James. I've been hearing all about your handsome nephew on my rounds.'

Alexander shook hands with the short, plump man, whose wide grin was emphasized by two magnificent sideburns that sat out like gills on his chubby face.

'So he simply had one dram too many, after all?' intervened Calum.

The doctor glanced mischievously at James. 'Will we tell them now, do you think, or wait until they witness the transformation for themselves?'

'What are you gibberin' about, man?' demanded Calum, impatient with the teasing.

'He claims to have *seen the light*,' declared James.

'My – oh my!' responded Calum. 'Now that would be somethin'.'

'Can I be let in on the joke?' asked Alexander.

'It's not really a joke,' explained James, 'although in Seorus's case, we have to suspect hallucinations. When people *see the light* in these parts, it means they've had a profound religious experience. Most islanders take it all very seriously.'

'What's he claiming to have seen?' snorted Alexander, incredulously.

'He's not saying exactly,' rejoined the doctor. 'But he's resolved to change his life.'

'I actually offered him a drink and he refused,' revealed James.

'Aye, many's the life that's altered course like that,' said Calum. 'Mind you, I know a few I preferred before the experience.'

'Were you born on Tora, Doctor?' asked Alexander.

'Almost – I came to live here when I was five, as my father then became the physician.'

'And glad we are of that, Martin,' James said, before turning to Calum and Alexander. 'How did your day go?'

'Grand, I'd say,' responded Calum. 'Everyone was glad to get a closer look at him. And your surprise guest for tonight met him in the village.'

'Since I did not remember her at first, it's probably fortunate,' Alexander added.

'I hope you'll provide some young male company for her, while you're here,' said James. 'She's had a hard time, poor girl.'

From warning him off Mhairi-Anne to match-making with Victoria, thought Alexander, his uncle was proving to be as great a trial as his father, but he said nothing as James added, 'The Reverend Morrison is coming, too, and Martin and his wife, Emily.'

'Quite a party!' observed Alexander.

'I'm looking forward to it,' the doctor assured, as he took his leave, 'and I'll take the opportunity to look in on my patient again.'

Alexander had not yet seen Seorus, when he joined the group in the dining-room, shortly before eight that evening, but as he entered, an unfamiliar voice was hailing the transformation in the patient as nothing short of a miracle.

'A more sober and chastened creature, I could not have hoped to see,' said the voice grandiloquently. 'You will be quite astounded, Victoria.'

Victoria's attention had been arrested by Alexander's entrance, however, and the speaker turned to ascertain the source of her distraction.

From his collar, it was apparent to Alexander that this was the Reverend Morrison, but his uncle immediately stepped forward to perform the introduction to him and the doctor's wife, while Alexander noted that Mhairi-Anne was yet missing from the party.

'You must come along to worship on Sunday,' said the minister almost at once. 'I'm sure the whole congregation will join with me in welcoming you.'

'I'll took forward to it,' agreed Alexander politely, before transferring his attention to the girl beside him, whose eyes, he knew, were fastened upon him. 'So nice to see you again, Victoria. You're looking splendid this evening.' Her brown hair was arranged immaculately in a more complex style than earlier in the day and she wore a demure, blue velvet gown that was pinched into her narrow waist and trimmed with a high pleated frill of lace around her delicate neck.

They were assembled in the area in front of the massive fire-place in the great dining-hall. Although they had dined there on Alexander's first evening on Tora, since then their meals had been taken in the adjacent breakfast-room, a less cavernous chamber, more suited to their normal number. The dimensions of the room made it one of the largest in the castle and it was also one of the most appealing. Its corner site allowed narrow leaded windows along two of its walls and its high ceiling was a masterpiece in stucco. A number of fine sixteenth-century tapestries adorned the stonework while an enormous oval table, currently resplendent in gleaming silverware, including two ornate candelabra, provided a focal point to the room. A matching oak sideboard, tall glass-fronted cabinet, occasional chairs and a *chaise-longue* positioned by the fireplace, where the guests lingered, completed the effect.

Above the fireplace hung a fine portrait of Elizabeth McNair, which Alexander had noticed on his first evening, without then taking an interest in the artist. Presently, however, he gazed with fresh interest, as he recognized the vibrancy of Mhairi-Anne's style. He turned to remark upon the painting, but found the Reverend Morrison again holding the floor on the topic of the divine visitation to Seorus Dhu. Impatient with Mhairi-Anne's absence and deprived of his moment to hail her talent, Alexander presumed to offer his own opinion on the 'miracle'.

'Isn't it a trifle premature to be taking this event so seriously, considering his abstinence has barely lasted a few hours?'

The minister, in his early forties, Alexander guessed, with a thick mane of chestnut-coloured hair, that was almost as eloquent as his expression, regarded him with barely disguised displeasure. His thin nose quivered, as if sniffing the air, and his pointed, self-righteous chin worked rapidly, while his indignation gave way to amused tolerance.

'Time is hardly the point in this matter, Alexander. That cannot be held up as a measure of God's hand. If Seorus fails, if his resolve weakens – that must not demean what happened here this very day.'

His lofty arrogance irked Alexander further. 'It seems to me that with his mind constantly lubricated by alcohol, he might be expected to see the odd vision.'

The minister, swiftly reminding himself who Alexander was,

managed a mirthless laugh. 'Indeed . . . indeed . . . we are all well acquainted with the habits of our very own Seorus Dhu. But the proximity of God to this isolated piece of land is also a well-documented phenomenon, which I daresay you, too, will acknowledge, if you deign to stay with us long enough. You will find. . . .'

He was now like a river in full spate, but as Alexander thought, with a sinking heart, that he had nobody to blame but himself, the door opened and Mhairi-Anne came in.

The reverend's voice faltered to a halt, as he realized the main recipient of his lecture was no longer receiving, but Alexander was scarcely aware of the awkward silence that marked her entrance. In a simple off-the shoulder gown of jade green that almost exactly matched her eyes, she was magnificent. His pulse raced at her effortless sensuality and the minister could have gone to Hell, as far as he was concerned.

The glow of the candles settled flatteringly over the party, as John and Flora proceeded to serve dinner, including delicious pickled herring, a joint of island lamb and bannocks. Dr Campbell, like Calum, was a mine of amusing stories, while Emily happily prompted one tale after another. Alexander's liking for the minister did not improve, as he had an irritating habit of steering every topic into a religious vein and he noticed that he virtually ignored Mhairi-Anne, while Victoria received much of his attention. As it had come to light that he was a bachelor, Alexander wondered if the girl might have found herself a suitor on Tora, after all.

Mhairi-Anne was seated diagonally across from Alexander and, try as he did, he could not keep his eyes from wandering in her direction, a fact which he feared Emily, seated next to him, had noticed, when she remarked to Victoria on his other side, 'A most fetching colour – Mhairi-Anne's gown – isn't it, Victoria?'

'Yes, but she would look well in anything,' responded Victoria with a wistful glance across the table. Then to Alexander, 'I saw you looking at her portrait of your aunt.'

'I had not realized she was the artist. It is even better than the one of Uncle James, I think. Are you an admirer of her work, Mrs Campbell?'

'Emily . . . please. Oh yes – credit where credit is due, she has a fine gift.'

Alexander was gratified to hear someone else praise Mhairi-Anne's work, although he sensed a certain reservation in her comment.

Quite suddenly, the minister joined their conversation. 'We'll be sending the portrait to Henry Jamieson to assist him in his work on the statue,' he said loudly across the table.

'I'm afraid I could not agree to that.'

Alexander glanced up the table to see Mhairi-Anne looking directly at Morrison, a determined expression on her face, although she had spoken quietly.

Other conversations were abandoned, as the reverend responded stridently, 'But it is agreed! Mr Jamieson requires a good likeness. 'When I was instructed to commission him to undertake the sculpture, I was advised of the portrait's availability.'

Before James could respond to the minister's nodding cue for verification, Mhairi-Anne retorted, 'I was not consulted in this and I regret I cannot allow the portrait to be used for a purpose of which I am certain Mrs McNair would have disapproved.'

'Come ... come, Mhairi-Anne,' intervened James, with a soothing smile at the startled faces of his guests. 'I did not think I needed to ask your permission, since it has become a fixture in the castle. It is, undoubtedly, the best likeness we have of Elizabeth.'

'We will discuss it another time, James,' she said tightly, aware of the uncomfortable hush in the room. Then, with a dignity and composure Alexander could only admire, she rose. 'I'll tell Flora that we are finished at table.'

The drawing-room, where after-dinner drinks were served, was also a large room but furnished in a more haphazard fashion, with armchairs, sofas of various sizes and occasional tables providing comfortable little nooks that encouraged the dispersal of a company. Choosing to be as far away from Morrison as possible, Alexander settled beside Victoria on a sofa near the trolley from which Flora and Mhairi-Anne were dispensing whisky, brandy or port. As he hoped, she eventually sat down in an armchair adjacent to them.

'We have not had a chance to talk all evening,' she said to Victoria. 'I intended to visit on Sunday, but ended up making crab soup.'

'And delicious it was, too,' remarked Alexander.

'You must give me the recipe. My cooking is still so very limited.'

'You underestimate yourself.'

'As you evidently do,' said Alexander. 'I've learned today you're an accomplished artist.'

'If I could paint as I would like, I might consider I had something to boast about.'

'They say a true artist is always tantalized by the discrepancy between imaginative conception and the reality of a finished piece,' remarked Victoria. 'I am certain you could acquire quite a following, if you were to promote your work on the mainland.'

'I would be happy to take some of your paintings back with me,' offered Alexander. 'My father has many contacts. . . .'

He stopped, as already she was shaking her head. 'My ambitions lie in self-satisfaction, not renown.' She paused, staring across at the Reverend Morrison, before murmuring, 'I'm sorry if I spoiled the atmosphere at dinner.'

'The man is a self-righteous prig!' muttered Alexander.

'You are brave and say what you think,' Victoria whispered. 'I wish I could be like that. But tell me, is my portrait completed yet?'

'All but the finishing touches.'

'You should do one of Alexander,' Victoria suggested impulsively, her voice halting suddenly, as instantly she regretted the idea. She had noticed how he had watched Mhairi-Anne all evening.

Alexander, however, was enthusiastic. 'A new challenge for you, Mhairi-Anne. Why not?'

'I think your uncle would prefer you to spend your time on Tora more profitably.'

'I've always meant to ask how you managed to paint Mrs McNair's portrait, after she died?' Victoria intervened.

'I had done a number of sketches of her while she was alive, although she never actually sat for me. The rest came from memory and after numerous failures.'

The Campbells and the Reverend Morrison, at this point, were rising to leave and Victoria said, 'I, too, must go. I don't wish to keep John up later than is necessary, considering he has such an early rise.'

'I take it the Campbells do not live in Castlebay?' queried Alexander.

'Their home is off the moorland track beyond the church.'

'So you're leaving, too?' said James, who now joined their group. 'Why don't you see Victoria home with John, Alexander? I'm sure she will welcome your company a little longer.'

Alexander was annoyed, as he had hoped to continue talking with Mhairi-Anne, but, in response to Victoria's protests, he was obliged to insist. The only saving grace in the arrangement was the satisfaction Alexander derived from the minister's tight-lipped expression, when he realized that Victoria was to have him as an escort.

Outside, it was pitch black and the lamps, which hung swaying on the dogcart, hardly seemed to relieve it at all. A low half-moon sliced the sea with a ribbon of silver light, but as they moved off from the castle, it was like penetrating an inky fog, and for a time they rattled along, huddled against one another and hushed into silence.

Eventually, Victoria murmured, 'I love the island, but I do find the nights eerie.'

Alexander found the enveloping blackness rather soothing. He had felt on edge all evening – wanting Mhairi-Anne, disliking Morrison, annoyed by his uncle and disturbed by Victoria's obvious attraction to him. Now he felt rather sorry for her and he said, 'You should, perhaps, consider returning to the mainland. I could make enquiries about accommodation, or—'

'There's no need. I have a place – a hunting lodge in Perth – and I discovered I was not left entirely penniless, despite what the papers said.' There was more than a hint of pride in her voice. 'But I'm not ready yet.' She paused. 'When will you return?'

'I'm not sure. A few weeks, perhaps.'

'James would have you stay longer, I'm sure.'

He smiled faintly in the darkness. 'My uncle expects too much, I fear.'

'But you like the island, don't you?'

'Yes . . .' His voice tailed to a halt, as he suppressed a momentary urge to confide in her.

'Your inheritance will be a great responsibility, but worthwhile, I think. That's what I'm seeking now – some purpose in life.'

'For a woman, that is usually a home and children.'

'But a husband must come first,' she murmured, her voice dropping to a whisper, as she realized the forward nature of this remark. She forced a jerky laugh, before adding lightly, 'And I am not likely to find him here!'

He was relieved to discern a few dim lights beginning to glow in the darkness. 'I believe we are nearly there.'

Outside the library, he took a lantern and helped her down, and while John proceeded further along the road to turn the dogcart, he walked with her to the side entrance to her apartments.

'You have been most kind,' she murmured, when she had opened her door and lit the lamp inside. As she looked up at him shyly, her brown eyes glistening in the light, he succumbed to an unspoken invitation to kiss her on the cheek – an impulse he regretted immediately when he noted her rapturous expression.

'I'll see you soon,' he muttered tightly, before walking away smartly.

When he arrived back at the castle, his guilty thoughts about Victoria were abruptly terminated, as he heard raised voices issuing clearly into the hallway from the drawing-room. Mhairi-Anne and his uncle were having a heated argument.

'You're behaving like a child over this,' James was declaring. 'You embarrassed me, provoked William Morrison and gave God knows what impression to everyone else.'

'Impressions!' echoed Mhairi-Anne. 'You used to value principles and you know as well as I do that this statue is about more than commemorating your wife.'

'I know no such thing!'

Alexander had frozen in the hallway, their words bombarding his ears.

'Oh James! Elizabeth would have laughed to scorn the idea of her image being erected in stone, while children still run barefoot about this island.'

'The islanders want it.'

'Neil Graham and William Morrison want it, you mean! They're using you, James. You must see that.' Her voice now sounded close to tears. 'Yet still I am expected to deliver my work to help in this shrine.'

'Your work! The canvas hangs in my house in a frame I bought and paid for.'

There was a moment of startled silence. Alexander held his breath.

Then her voice rose again, so dangerously low, he could scarcely hear. 'It will not hang there much longer. Take comfort in that!'

The door to the room swung open so suddenly, Alexander staggered backwards into the shadows, while she banged it angrily behind her. For several seconds, she stood, chest heaving and head bowed, unaware that he was near. The castle was now eerily quiet around them and she started visibly, when he moved to make his presence known. Tears stood in her eyes and he went towards her instinctively, as her ravaged expression gave way rapidly to surging defiance. She actually smiled at him now, although he noticed her lips trembled still. Both caught in a mood of dangerous intensity, their kiss was as inevitable as time. Their mouths met, greedily open, while their bodies drew hard together in a stranglehold of arms; for several seconds they soared mindlessly on a savage hurricane of lust that consumed all reservation.

It ended as suddenly as it began, however. He emerged from the thoughtless compulsion of the moment – startled by the strength of the hands that pushed him away violently. A look of bewildered panic now engaged her, while he was voiceless, trying to bring his body under control. Before he could speak, she fled past him, the skirt of her gown bobbing and rustling with her agitation.

He dared not call out and could not follow in his present state. This, he endeavoured to alleviate by bending over, hands fixed hard to his knees to relieve the constraining pressure of his clothes. And it was thus his uncle found him, as he opened the sitting-room door. Too late to move, he closed his eyes with a soft curse and thought rapidly.

'Alexander – something wrong?' James sounded disgustingly normal, as he moved forward.

Alexander eased himself to his full height, his face grimacing. 'A touch of indigestion, I think. A spasm, no more. I'm fine now.'

'Victoria home safe?'

He nodded. 'I think I'll get to bed now.'

James moved with him towards the stairs. 'She's a lovely girl, don't you think?'

'Yes – but a trifle quiet for my taste.'

'You hardly know her yet.'

'I tend to be governed by first impressions.'

'Don't be. I'm sure there's more to her than meets the eye.'

His body still throbbing with discomfort, Alexander responded frustratedly, 'I thought it was Tora that I was supposed to fall in love with, Uncle.'

'I merely thought she might provide you with some suitable company.' They had now reached the top of the stairs where they would part for their respective rooms.

'Instead of Mhairi-Anne!'

At the mention of her name, James's eyes became evasive and he shrugged. 'I'm tired, m'boy. Time I was in bed.'

Little wonder after such a quarrel, Alexander thought, as he proceeded thankfully to his own room.

The quarrel itself, however, did not occupy Alexander's thoughts, as it might have done, but for the memorable kiss that had followed it. Instead, he savoured over and over those few unbelievable seconds, when instinct had triumphed over every convention. This was the breakthrough he had wanted. Yet, he could not rid himself of a strange sense of foreboding that tainted his exultation, until the pink glow of dawn light crept stealthily into his room.

CHAPTER FIVE

ALEXANDER'S sense of foreboding proved justified, when, far from being a breakthrough, that night marked a definite deterioration in his relationship with Mhairi-Anne. Generally, she avoided him like a nasty cold; she never allowed any opportunity for him to catch her alone; and the only indication that she had any recollection of their memorable kiss was in her strict avoidance of any eye contact with him at meal times. Clearly, she was embarrassed that he had caught her in a moment of unguarded passion and wished to forget all about it, while the memory haunted his thoughts like a scene from an accident, replayed over and over again.

A few times in his life, he had thought he might be in love, but, ironically now, he did not dwell on this possibility, perhaps because he did not wish to contemplate the dire implications of such a happening. He had only known the woman five minutes, he told himself disparagingly, any time this thought threatened to develop in his mind. But he *was* obsessed with her! That he could not deny. Every morning he rose with the hope of seeing her alone; every night his sleep was restless and disturbed by his frustration, so much so that Calum remarked several times on the shadows underlining his eyes at the breakfast-table. By contrast, there was no lasting coolness evident between James and Mhairi-Anne. Their quarrel appeared swiftly forgotten; the portrait of his aunt remained *in situ*; and Alexander could only conclude that, like his father and him, they could have nasty disagreements that were rapidly overtaken by more important considerations.

As the days marched into weeks, and his desire became a mania that tormented his thoughts and stung relentlessly in his blood, he even began wondering, at times, if there could be anything in the superstitious beliefs about her. Calum had said that she had a powerful effect on people and certainly he felt bewitched! Now, he could credit how a boy might easily topple from a cliff, if his mind was thus distracted, or a man fall overboard in a moment of crazy carelessness. He knew he should leave the island – he even wished fervently that he had never come – but he could not contemplate abandoning the place without some resolution of this terrible derangement of his normal state. When a letter arrived from his father, approving of his decision to remain on Tora, he was, therefore, gratified, even though Sir David spent several paragraphs warning him to keep a clear head with regard to the harsh realities of his uncle's 'dream' island.

The transformation in Seorus Dhu proved to be no fleeting phase and he emerged from his sickbed a much altered creature. Gone was his inimitable foolish grin and his large eyes no longer rolled like loose marbles in his head. Most amazingly, his navigational skills improved and he could walk in an almost straight line between two points, albeit with a slight limp. He also now offered reasonably sensible responses, considering he had been portraying himself as a simpleton for years. Alexander put it all down to his continuing abstinence from alcohol, but all over Tora, he was hailed as God's handiwork.

April gave way to May and the weather continued unseasonably mild. The sowing of crops which had begun in March with oats, had been followed by planting of potatoes, barley and corn. Turnips, flax, hemp and other necessary crops were also grown in lesser quantities and James explained to Alexander the necessity for regular rotation of what was grown in each section of the land, in order to produce the best possible yields each year.

Seaweed was gathered from the shore in large creels that the islanders carried on their backs, to supplement the animal manure needed to encourage strong growth. In his frequent rides over the island, sometimes alone, often with James or Calum, Alexander saw in use a variety of agricultural implements: the *cas-chrom*, or crooked spade; several different types of hoes; a racan, used for breaking up sods and a one-handled wooden plough pulled by two horses. With the sowing of crops completed, an annual migration of most of the animals to the summer pasture beneath Mount Tora was soon to be initiated, so that none of the growth would be devoured by hungry beasts. Meantime, watchmen were appointed in each village to keep an eye open for cattle, sheep or goats straying on to the cultivated land, and people talked eagerly of the operation involved in removing their animals to the Mount Tora ground – a lively festival-type event, by all accounts.

On the second Sunday in May, a freak summer day enveloped Tora. The wind, a perpetual feature of the weather, as Alexander knew it, vanished and the sky was a misty canopy of blue over the ocean, which, uncharacteristically, was as calm as a pond. The air was hot as they ambled the short distance back to the castle from church, Victoria walking beside Alexander, while Calum and James came on behind, a habit which had developed since Alexander had been persuaded that he should appear in the kirk. In fact, he had seen a good deal more of Victoria than he deemed sensible, considering he was well aware of the girl's infatuation with him, but his uncle had an unfortunate habit of contriving to make arrangements for them in her presence and in his current beleaguered state of mind, he never seemed able to think quickly enough to extricate himself without offending her. Thus, she had dined regularly at the castle; they had met weekly at church, which invariably led on to Sunday afternoon excursions; she had the uncanny knack of appearing at the library door any time he was in the village, and they had been riding together over the island several times. Had his relationship with Mhairi-Anne been progressing satisfactorily, he would have chosen some moment to make his lack of interest gently evident to her. As things were, however, it was all too easy to derive a modicum of comfort from her company and obvious admiration.

'Seorus walks remarkably well now,' said Victoria. Seorus, John and Flora were some way ahead of them on the path from church. 'It's hard to credit he's the same man.'

'His transformation has the appearance of a miracle, I must admit.'

'William . . . that is the Reverend Morrison tells me that he is to address the congregation soon. Apparently it is the custom when someone *sees the light*.'

'Poor Seorus!' muttered Alexander, deciding that the unfortunate creature would appear like some exhibit on display, for the glorification of Morrison's opinion.

'You still do not share our minister's conviction in the event.'

'I'm afraid he and I have little in common.' His enthusiasm for Morrison had not improved, now he was obliged to listen every Sunday to his boring diatribes on the Hell and damnation that awaited anyone, who chanced to enjoy life.

'Alexander, there is something I would like to discuss with you. I need advice—' Her urgently whispered words were cut short, as James and Calum caught up with them outside the castle.

'You'll join us for lunch, Victoria?' invited James immediately.

'It's such a lovely day, I thought to take a picnic to the beach.'

'An excellent idea! I'm sure you'd enjoy an afternoon in the sunshine too, Alexander.'

With Victoria looking even more eager than usual for his company, he complied.

'Come then,' said James. 'I'll arrange for Flora to put your luncheon into a basket.'

'I've a feelin' we'll be payin' a price for this little piece of summer,' Calum predicted, as they all proceeded towards the castle.

'Your bunion playing up, Calum?'

'Like the devil.'

'But no call for pessimism on a day like this,' retorted James cheerfully.

'Nature gives nothin' for nothin'. You mark my words!'

They settled in a deep sand dune, fronting the beach where he had walked with Mhairi-Anne and, remembering that this interlude had been overlooked, he was glad to note that the high sides and deep grassland afforded utter privacy from prying eyes, unless these peered through a telescope from the summit of Mount Tora. He felt that he had already been seen too often in the company of Victoria and he did not want to add a cosy picnic for two to the list of their assignations probably sweeping the island from the post office.

Victoria proceeded to set out their lunch, which included a fine bottle of wine from James's cellar, while he lay chewing on a blade of grass, staring out over the deserted sand and sheet of ocean, thinking that if Mhairi-Anne had been his companion, he might have deemed himself in heaven. They ate and drank, speaking only spasmodically, as she seemed to sense something of his mood of despondency. Eventually, however, he recalled that she had wanted advice – about her return to the mainland – he was hoping. But it was another matter entirely.

'I've . . . I've had a proposal of marriage,' she revealed hesitantly.

He was surprised, but knew immediately from whom. 'Our minister?'

She nodded. 'We dined together last evening.'

'I take it, you're not certain of your answer.'

'He has given me a week to make up my mind.'

Typical, thought he, an ultimatum! And he feared he knew why she was seeking his counsel. He could see in the nervous anxiety of her face and her movements that this was really about him, not William Morrison. She wanted his dissuasion.

'You obviously do not love him, otherwise you would have no dilemma,' he eventually offered carefully.

'But I would not be the first to opt for marriage for practical reasons. Given my situation, I feel I should consider it.'

'Yes.'

The solitary word of encouragement wounded her. She looked down evasively at a napkin she was wringing in her hands, before she murmured, 'So you think, it might be wise?'

A vision of her fragile spirit being crushed on the altar of Morrison's narrow-minded dictates swept over him and he sat forward, embracing his knees, as he said tightly, 'I think you are too young to settle for security without the promise of happiness. You're less than half his age and, to be frank, I do not like the man.'

'You would not advise it, then.' The relief in her voice was palpable.

'I'm not an authority, Victoria,' he said, after finishing his wine in one hasty swallow.

'But you think I should delay?'

Feeling trapped, he suddenly turned like a wounded animal and said bluntly, 'You should return to the mainland as soon as possible. There, you may meet someone suitable.' The cruel intensity of his gaze now obviated any need for him to add that he was not that person.

Her eyes fled moistly from his, as she responded in a voice he could scarcely hear, 'I will be more lonely than ever on the mainland.'

As she buried her nose in a handkerchief and her shoulders quivered, he lay back helplessly on the tartan rug they had laid out and gazed up at the canopy of blue sky, where seagulls winged in enviable freedom. He felt cornered, but so was she. If she did not marry Morrison, her prospects were bleak. Even on the mainland, suitors of her class would not be lining up to link their names to a girl of such notoriety, particularly as her relations did not seem to want to know her either.

'I am such a fool,' she muttered disdainfully, her back to him as she tossed her handkerchief aside. Turning her head then, she glanced down at him. 'You must think I have no pride at all.'

He gazed deliberately still at the sky. 'That's not true! I should have. . . .' His voiced tailed to a halt, as she was suddenly leaning over him.

'. . . Told me you are in love with Mhairi-Anne?'

Startled by her precocity, he muttered evasively, 'I'm not sure how I feel about her – and, of course, there are other considerations.'

'Does she love you?' she queried, gazing at him over the rim of her wine glass, the alcohol lending her uncustomary boldness.

He cradled his head in his hands as he squinted up at her, a cynical smile playing on his lips. 'You use that word with such certainty. I'm not sure I know what it means and I have no idea how she feels about me.'

Having set her empty glass aside, she turned on to her stomach, so that they lay now facing each other, the sky framing the dark brown of her hair.

He was instantly aware of the intimacy which suddenly enveloped them. If he moved his hands, he would touch her; if he sat up, he would need to thrust her aside.

'I love you!' she whispered, her voice shaking with intensity. 'I love you!' Even as tremors of warning raced through his body, her mouth descended fervently on his and the tip of his tongue betrayed his involuntary arousal by instinctively tracing the seam of her innocent lips, so that they opened invitingly.

Now he did move, however, exclaiming angrily, as she was inevitably rolled on to her back, 'This is madness . . . madness!'

'Please . . . Alexander.' Her hands clutched at his jacket. 'If I am to marry Morrison – or someone like him – I don't want to wait for that.'

His fingers now circled her wrists, poised to free himself. 'You're . . . you're . . . upset. You don't know what you're saying. It's the wine—'

'I love you!' she interjected vehemently. 'I know you don't love me, but you . . . you must want me, don't you?'

Later – this moment became the zenith of his self-recriminations: the moment he should have stopped – but didn't; the moment he allowed himself to be drawn into the same precarious pool of emotion in which she was drowning; the moment when all of his frustration of past weeks found a willing, attractive substitute for his ungovernable lust for Mhairi-Anne. With an unintelligible curse, born both of protest and submission, he slowly descended on her.

With the wine warming their blood, it was all too easy to be swept along on her love and his misplaced passion and he ravaged the innocence of her lips, until she was moaning in incoherent desire, while he moved inexorably beyond rational thought. Overhead, the sky remained a relentless, unseeing blue – blind to the gruelling, mindless intimacy which stormed over them in rolling waves of sensation, unleashed in muffled cries of wonder and relief. When it was finally over, they lay side by side, heaving thickly into the incredulous silence, which followed.

Fifteen minutes later, they had still not spoken a word. He now sat, arms supported on his knees, holding his head, unable to believe what he had done. She still lay on her back, clothes again in place, but no other evidence that she had even moved.

His self-remonstrations reached a climax when he suddenly sprang to his feet to savour the wind that had risen around them, wishing it could somehow miraculously blow away, like sand, all recollection of what he had done. He could not yet begin to comprehend the diabolical nature of the passion that had overtaken him. In a legal sense, he knew it was not rape, but in a moral sense, he was guilty as the Devil. He had violated her in a manner that was utterly abhorrent to him now and there was only one way he could begin to pay penance for it. He turned at the feel of her hand on his shoulder and saw the evidence of his assault: her lustrous brown hair blew freely in the wind and her lips were bruised a vivid pink from his kisses.

'We'll get married,' he said softly.

She smiled briefly, but was already shaking her head. 'You're not to blame. I won't marry you for this. You'd end up hating me.'

'How can you say that after what I've done?' he demanded. 'I must marry you. I will!'

She shook her head vehemently now. 'It was my fault – not yours.' She shrugged and sighed deeply. 'Besides, I do not regret it. I wanted to know what I'll be missing all of my life. I did not expect anything beyond a memory.'

'You deserve better!'

'Perhaps, but I know now I will not marry William Morrison, or any other man I do not love. You think this was a mistake, but, in a way, you have done me a favour. I might have made a much more serious error, had I blundered into a loveless union.' As the wind began to whip along the shore in front of them, she added, 'Come – we will need to pack up.'

Victoria having tucked her hair underneath her straw hat, he lifted the basket and they set off back over the moorland track in silence, Alexander still torn between what he knew he ought to do – and what he wanted to do. When they came to a fork in the track, she suddenly indicated her intention to follow the alternative route to the village.

'You will be expected at the castle.'

'Make some excuse.'

'My proposal still stands. You must think about it.'

She shook her head briefly, but firmly. 'You will not pay the price for my foolishness and you must forget all about it.' She moved away from him swiftly, while he stood still, knowing that if he tried hard enough, he might convince her, but she did not look back. He watched her until she was out of sight, before he resumed his course to the castle. The heat, as yet unrelieved by the wind, held the promise of thunder and his legs felt like dead weights, while his heart pounded with unrelenting remorse. He had made love to many women, but never had he taken advantage of the vulnerability of an innocent girl.

By the time he reached the castle, he felt quite ill and he hoped fervently to escape to his room without notice. Of all people, however, Mhairi-Anne was crossing the hall as he entered, and her footsteps faltered when she saw him. 'What is the matter? You look unwell.'

He laid the picnic basket down, an unreasoning fury welling up in his chest. Recently, she had been sweeping past him with barely a word. Now, of all times, she chose to show concern! As he gritted his teeth against the unjustifiable blame he suddenly wanted to hurl upon her, she asked, 'Will I call your uncle?'

'No!' He managed to take hold of himself. 'I have a headache. Tell him I won't be down for dinner. I'm going to bed.'

'Where is Victoria? Is she all right?'

'Of course! Why wouldn't she be?' he demanded, coldly.

'Would you like something sent up to your room?'

'No!' He could not bear the anxiety in her eyes any longer and he moved swiftly towards the stairs, calling over his shoulder, 'See the basket is returned to Flora, if you will.'

In his room, he headed immediately for an unopened bottle of brandy residing in his luggage. He consumed two measures in rapid gulps. Then he locked his door and, loosening his tie, he sat down in the armchair by the fire, kicked off his boots, and, at a more leisurely pace, set about the task of getting himself thoroughly drunk.

CHAPTER SIX

DESERVEDLY, he surfaced the next morning with a colossal hangover. He lay now on top of his bed, but wore still the clothes of yesterday. Every nerve in his body seemed to cry for assistance and as an avalanche of fresh recollection engulfed him, so did a wave of nausea. He leapt from his bed to retch.

He raised his head from the bowl some minutes later, his ears only now attuning to sounds in the room. The chimney was roaring and spitting soot on to the hearth and the windows were shivering in their frames. As a squall of hail gusted against the panes, he rallied to investigate.

An icy blast of air hit his face when he opened the window a mere fraction. He gasped, staring incredulously at the scene which greeted him. The blue sea of the day before had been transformed into a churning grey mass, with waves being hurled against the harbour wall in mountainous spume. The sky was a leaden charcoal and a rumble of thunder was followed by a jagged streak of lightning, which zig-zagged across the sky, like a whip. He tugged the window shut and sought his pocket watch. It was after nine o'clock. He would have some explaining to do, he thought with a groan.

Having doused himself in a pitcher of ice-cold water, washed, shaved and changed, he was able to present himself downstairs. To his surprise, he found Mhairi-Anne seated alone with a cup of tea at the breakfast-table. The normal breakfast buffet had been removed.

She made to rise. 'I'll tell Flora you're here.'

He shook his head. 'I don't want anything – just coffee.'

'The pot is still hot.'

He poured himself a cup and joined her.

'Are you feeling better?'

'Much,' he lied.

'James was worried about you. He knocked on your door, but you were apparently asleep.'

'I'm sorry, I was so abrupt with you last night,' he murmured guiltily.

'It's of no matter.'

'Is there no school today?'

'Owing to the weather, only three of the children appeared. I sent them home as it was obviously getting worse. Calum and your uncle are gone to the harbour to make sure all the fishing boats are back safely.' She sighed. 'Calum predicted we would pay for our little piece of summer.'

He smiled faintly. 'His bunion!' Then remembering how he had spent the afternoon, he sobered, laying his cup down and rubbing his eyes.

'You're still not well,' she remarked.

He gazed at her, thinking she seemed more beautiful with every day that passed. If only it had been her.

Something in his eyes betrayed his thoughts. She suddenly stood up. 'I must go.'

'You're afraid to be alone with me since that night.'

She looked momentarily startled that he had dared to broach the subject. 'That night – I was upset,' she said carefully. 'What happened, never would have happened otherwise.'

'It was waiting to happen!' he retorted.

She laughed nervously. 'Destiny? You forget. I do not conform to God, or destiny, for that matter.'

'Perhaps, you'll find you have no more choice in the matter than any of us,' he said, a note of bitterness creeping into his voice.

'Everyone has a choice,' she murmured, before closing the door softly behind her.

Yes – he had certainly had a choice yesterday, he thought dismally, but it had still happened against all the odds and all his feelings, on a freak summer day, when he had wanted only to be with her. If his behaviour had been down to destiny, perhaps, he could begin to forgive himself. With no choice, there need be no guilt.

As voices in the hallway heralded the return of Calum and James, he rose to go and greet them, not wishing to explain his lack of appetite. They were both wearing enormous oilskins that dripped water all over the stone floor. Mhairi-Anne was with them and they were evidently agitated.

'Any word of a boat being beached at Port nam Magan?' asked James.

Mhairi-Anne shook her head.

'The Stewarts' boat is missing.'

'Is that the family we visited near Murran?' asked Alexander, recalling a cheerful man with an equally cheerful brood of sons.

'Aye – and all seven of them are aboard,' said Calum. 'His wife was down by the harbour. They're goin' now to the Point to take a look and I guess she'll be along with them.'

'I think we'll head there, too, Calum,' said James. 'I'll not rest, waiting for news.'

'I'll come as well,' said Alexander, his own troubles seeming suddenly insignificant by comparison to this.

James only now seemed to recall he had been ill. 'Headache gone now, is it?'

Alexander nodded, realizing he had avoided any awkward questions due to this emergency.

James clapped him on the back. 'You might as well see Tora at her worst.'

'I'll come, too,' Mhairi-Anne suggested suddenly.

James glanced back at her. 'You'd better stay here, in case there's news from elsewhere.'

Dressed in another oilskin, Alexander climbed into the rear seat of the dogcart, beside his uncle, while Calum drove up front. 'She could have had shelter here between us,' he said. 'It's a pity to leave her worrying alone.'

James shook his head. 'Then if anything goes wrong out here, she'd be the bad luck that caused it.

'You can't be serious?'

'Grief's easier to bear if you can blame somebody, lad. Let's not tempt fate.'

The ferocious gale roaring unimpeded over the moorland was daunting.

'Are we safe in this contraption?' yelled Alexander, competing with the wind for audibility.

'If it tilts too far – jump!' James shouted back.

Several times during the journey, he was poised to launch himself into space, but somehow the vehicle righted itself and the plucky horse, head low, fought the gale like a tiny warrior. He had never experienced a storm like it. Gorse and bush were crushed, debris was activated to frantic whirling life, and the moorland looked as if God was in the process of ironing out its every bump or crease. Squalls of hail and sleet broke out like spasmodic gunfire and streaks of lightning continued to whip the sky in angry white lashes.

Adversity, he discovered, did wonders for a hangover. As he braced himself against the elemental sinews of nature at her worst, constantly assessing and reassessing the need to leap for his life, his headache vanished in rushes of undiluted fear.

When he saw the scene at Tora Point, he was reminded of Neil Graham's words to him on the ferry. The spray from the ocean rose over them, salting the heavy rain, and the waves were awesome, mobile cliffs that swelled to white-tipped crescendos to batter the land in furious white foam.

Mrs Stewart was already there, surrounded by a group of fishermen, but at first they could see nothing more than the primitive raging of the sea. It was Calum who spotted the boat first, rising like a barrel from the mouth of oblivion. Then others spotted her. There was a clamour of excitement, mixed with anxiety. Apart from the imminent and constant danger of her being swamped and capsized, there was also the more insidious peril of her being sucked in a chasm against the pulverizing force of the cliffs. Why had they not headed for the sanctuary of Port nam Magan, Alexander asked Calum?

'Beachin' a boat there in fine weather is easy enough,' Calum shouted, above the roaring of the waves, 'but there are rocks round that beach and the currents will be fierce today.'

'But they'd be able to get ashore, even if they did bottom her,' Alexander yelled back.

'Aye – but there's more than life and limb at stake here. They need the earnin' power of their boat and old Alistair isn't about to risk their livelihood, if there's a chance of gettin' her in whole.'

Alexander noticed that every time the boat vanished, Mrs Stewart's hands fastened in a mute prayer, until, miraculously, the vessel was regurgitated, like superfluous food spat out by the greedy sea. They watched helplessly, as this cruel game was enacted over and over again in front of their waiting eyes.

Almost an hour passed, before the spray washing over them thinned to a mist. The wind was dropping. Cautious excitement rippled through their ranks, as they eagerly anticipated progress. The boat laboured still for several minutes. Then, abruptly, as if God had unleashed a restraining anchor, she was on her way.

There was much emotion and roars of triumph on the cliff top. Alexander, too, was embraced and whirled around by the joyous wife. And he knew that had the outcome been different, he would have felt her grief as surely as he shared her jubilation.

The journey back to the castle was considerably less hazardous and he and James fell into silence. Alexander had wished a hundred times the day before that he had never set foot on this island, but the drama he had just witnessed made him think again. He was learning here about life and himself, faster than he had ever done on the mainland. Cocooned in idle affluence, he had never known a moment of real anxiety, misery, or true happiness for that matter, before he had come to Tora. But here it was all possible, he thought. Here he was growing as an individual and although he did not like the discovery of his fallibility of yesterday, perhaps even that was better than ignorant stagnation?

'I'll have to go to Inverness soon to get this Port nam Magan project underway,' James suddenly communicated, as they rattled into the castle courtyard. 'If the Stewarts had gone down out there, I'd never have forgiven myself for dawdling on raising that pier.'

'What's in Inverness?' asked Alexander.

'The builders – the planners. If someone doesn't put some pressure on them to get the drawings finalized, materials ordered and dates set, we could still be waiting this time next year to start.'

'When will you go?'

He shrugged. 'It will take about a week and I wouldn't want to leave during your visit.'

'Calum's here. Don't let me stop you.'

'We'll see,' said James thoughtfully. 'How did your picnic go by the way?'

Alexander felt as if he had been dropped from a great height. 'It was all very pleasant,' he muttered through his teeth.

The following morning, James was at breakfast alone with his nephew, when a recorded letter arrived for him.

'Well, that's that settled!' said James, as Alexander looked up to see him scrutinizing the communication. 'I'll have to go to Inverness now.'

'What's happened?'

'Elizabeth's father has died. He lived with us here for a time after we were married, but he suffered from dementia. Eventually, I had to put him in a sanatorium in Inverness some years back.' He shook his head reflectively. 'Must be all of seventy-nine, by now, but he had a strong heart.'

'You'll have to go to the funeral?' Alexander deduced.

'And make all the arrangements, by the look of it. He'll have to be buried there beside her mother. This is too bad!'

'I'm sorry to hear it, Uncle.'

'Oh – I can't pretend any great grief over him, m'boy! The way he was, he's better away. But I'll need to leave you to your own devices.'

'I told you yesterday not to mind me. See to the funeral and your business.' He smiled reassuringly. 'I won't slip away in your absence.'

'No,' agreed James, nodding thoughtfully. 'And Calum's here to keep an eye on things. I'd better go and see him.'

Alexander continued eating his breakfast, guiltily relieved to be granted this breathing space, when his relationship with Victoria could be rendered all the more awkward by his uncle's match-making.

CHAPTER SEVEN

By the time Alexander rose the following morning, James had already left on a specially arranged ferry, but he found Calum awaiting him in the breakfast-room with a busy schedule planned for their day, overseeing work necessitated all over the island, in the wake of Monday's storm.

The timing of the storm had, in fact, been fortuitous, according to Calum. A month later and crops would have been ruined. As things were, much was still below ground; the perpetual wind would soon dry out the saturated land, and more sowing could be undertaken to replace any young growth that had been damaged.

Structural damage had been suffered by almost every family, however; the castle stables had been partially demolished and the roof on the schoolhouse had been rent asunder. The consequence of this was that the children had been given an unexpected two-week holiday, while repairs were initiated, and everyone would now be frantically busy, trying to make good the damage to their crofts, before they became involved in the annual migration of their animals to the summer pastures.

Alexander spent much time in the saddle that day, riding from croft to croft, on Calum's instructions, assessing how repairs were progressing and taking notes of materials or equipment needed, for which James would ultimately foot the bill through his insurance company. Feeling needed and being useful was still a novel experience he enjoyed, and he was glad to have his mind thus occupied by practical considerations, which lifted him out of the quagmire of guilt that still awaited him in quieter moments. He returned to the castle, hungry, for the first time since Sunday afternoon, and, as always, looking forward to seeing Mhairi-Anne at dinner.

Almost at once, he sensed that she was in a strange mood. One minute, she was laughing and conversing in a more carefree manner than ever; the next, she was lost from the conversation, her expression melancholy and oddly dangerous.

In one of her lighter moments, she made a suggestion, which surprised and delighted him.

'I've decided I would like to paint your portrait after all, Alexander, now the school is closed, if you are still inclined to sit for me.'

'But of course!'

'We will start tomorrow morning, then.'

'He has things to do with me!'

Alexander turned at the sharpness in Calum's tone. 'We've finished the most urgent assessments.'

'Aye – but there's plenty else to do.'

'How long will it take, Mhairi-Anne?' asked Alexander, irritated by the dourness of Calum's attitude.

'An hour, no more, for a first sitting,' she said tightly.

'I can spare that, surely, Calum?'

'You do as you please!'

Alexander shrugged and looked at Mhairi-Anne, but she was gazing down at her plate, avoiding eye contact with both of them.

As Calum quite often went to bed directly after dinner, Alexander thought he might not linger with them, but he was as perverse as Mhairi-Anne that evening and silently followed in their wake. They were all passing through the adjoining dining-hall on their way to the drawing-room, when Alexander glanced back. Calum was staring fixedly at the wall above the great fireplace. The portrait of Elizabeth McNair had vanished.

Mhairi-Anne was already starting to pour coffee, when they arrived in the drawing-room.

'What's happened to your painting?' asked Calum immediately.

She did not look up from her task. 'James took it with him to Inverness. He intends to pay a visit to Henry Jamieson while he is there.'

'He told you that, did he?'

'John did,' she murmured with a brittle smile, as she handed him a cup of coffee.

As Alexander took his cup, he felt certain that she was furious with his uncle and wondered if this was behind her strange mood and her fresh interest in him. Was it possible that James had previously issued a warning to her, as he had to him, and now she was set to ignore the advice, as he had evidently ignored her wishes about the painting? The kiss had come after their quarrel: now this offer to paint his portrait. It all seemed to make sense. The more he tried to keep them apart, the more they were both resenting his dictates – especially, when it seemed he could please himself what he did. He had no business interfering, in any case. Look where it had led with Victoria. . . .

After coffee, he was disappointed when she indicated her intention to retire for the night and Calum stoically chaperoned them to the last. However, a time was arranged for his first sitting the next morning and he went to bed in a cheerful frame of mind, shrugging off thoughts of Sunday afternoon. He had asked Victoria to marry him: she had refused. He simply could not go on punishing himself.

Mhairi-Anne's studio was a room at the rear of the castle, which had once been used by Elizabeth McNair as a sewing-room, for the same reason that Mhairi-Anne had chosen it – a large square window that afforded ample daylight.

The session the following morning started out badly, when the first thing Alexander noticed on entering was Victoria's portrait standing against one wall. Despite his resolution of the night before, as he stared at it, he was beset by a vicious spasm of guilt and annoyed that her image would haunt this time with Mhairi-Anne.

'You've made her look quite beautiful,' he remarked stiffly, as Mhairi-Anne proceeded to arrange some sketching paper on a board.

'She is beautiful, I think, although on first meeting that is, perhaps, not so apparent.' She stopped to gaze across at the portrait thoughtfully. 'I feel sorry for her, left as she is. She is too gentle for this world, I fear.'

He turned his back on the portrait. 'Has she seen it yet?'

'Yes, she was very pleased. John is to take it to her on his next trip to the village. In fact, I will place it over here, so that I can complete the packaging.'

He was relieved to see the portrait being placed on a table, out of his view.

'Now we can get started. This morning, I only want to do some preliminary sketches from different angles. Will you sit in that chair by the window and spread one arm along the sill?'

For the next half-hour, she was all too intent upon producing a series of rough sketches and eventually, he said, 'My neck is getting stiff. Could we have a break?'

'I think we'll try it with more profile,' she murmured, as he exercised his neck.

'Do you always start with charcoal sketches?'

'Yes – then I paint, when I think I have the composition right.'

'You must be angry with my uncle?'

She stiffened at his abrupt change of subject, but made no verbal response.

'My father has a nasty habit of doing precisely as he pleases, too, when he tires of an argument.'

'I don't want to discuss this, Alexander.'

He shrugged and she approached him with an air of purpose. 'I think I have it now. We'll have your arm like so and the chair a little closer to the window, so there's more light and shadow on your face.' While these manoeuvres were enacted, she touched him lightly and he tensed like a spring. Her hand lingered on his chin, as she tilted his head slightly. 'There – that's much better, but turn your eyes towards me.'

'That will not be an arduous task.'

'You have the most remarkable eyes, you know. The colour changes with the light.'

He laughed. 'My mother has a jewel which does that. But if you're saying my eyes are like jewels, I might suspect you're flirting with me.'

'I'm an artist, not a flirt. And I must capture that expression, of course!'

'What expression?'

'Oh – you have the look of a predator, I think. Any moment I expect you to pounce.'

'Like this!' He suddenly leapt to his feet, drawn by a force that was now working headily between them.

'Now you have moved!' she admonished him, but as she looked up at him, her expression belied the reprimand.

'What colour are my eyes now?'

'Dark . . . very dark.'

'Why is that do you suppose?'

'Your face is in shadow.'

'Nothing to do with my mood?'

'We should get started.'

'You, too, have striking eyes.'

'They are too narrow.'

'Sensual! And beautiful . . . beautiful lips.' He moved closer.

'We . . . we must get started, while the light is good.'

'Yes – we must . . .' Their bodies now touched and he felt a delicious triumph in the knowledge that this was a mutual attraction.

'I see now, the look I wish to capture,' she murmured. 'The villain, the scoundrel, the bite beneath your cloak of charm.'

He laughed softly, so close to her now, he could feel the soft warmth of her breath. 'You do not intend to flatter me.'

As his arms went round her, her playful smile faded. She gasped audibly as he kissed first the sensitive skin of her neck. The assurance of her arousal intoxicated him and every taste of her seemed liked a luscious sin. Her cheeks, her temples, her hair – all were plundered in an exquisite journey of discovery that led to her lips. The wanton thrust of sensations stirring his blood exploded then into a primitive urge to bear her down and they subsided on to the battered couch behind them, oblivious to its shrieking protests. Their mouths revelled in the most intimate intercourse, their tongues interacting in a tunnel of dark delight. His hands were working skilfully with the small buttons on her dress, when the knocking came upon the door.

A disbelieving curse escaped his lips.

'Mr McNair, I must speak to you.'

'It's John!' she hissed, struggling away from him and calling out, 'Wait a moment, John, please!'

Having patted agitatedly at her hair and run her fingers over the ravaged buttons of her dress, she went and opened the door with remarkable composure, while Alexander sat forward on the couch, elbows supported on his knees to conceal his arousal.

'Is something wrong, John?' she asked.

'Mr MacRitchie's had an accident.'

Alexander managed to stand. 'Not serious, I trust?'

'He's hurt his ankle and wants to see you right away, Mr McNair.'

'Tell him, I'll be along directly.'

As soon as the servant departed, he caught her in his arms once more.

'We can't go on like this. I felt like strangling the poor man.'

'You must go and see Calum.'

'I have a feeling this is something of a hoax. Calum is against us, I fear.'

'The world is against us,' she murmured soberly.

He paused, kissing her face before he whispered, 'Will you

come to my room tonight?'

She was silent for a tantalizing moment. 'You come to my room. It is further away from Calum.'

He squeezed her hard against him in a paroxysm of delight. 'I love you! Oh, how I love you!' The words came to his lips, unbidden, and a surprised pause ensued.

'What is it? What's wrong?' he asked, noting her eyes were suddenly moist.

'You must say that to every woman you want to bed,' she murmured, cynically.

He smiled guiltily. 'I've never meant it before.'

'But you mean it now?'

'You don't believe me?'

'Love is hard to find and even harder to keep. Let's not fool each other, Alexander.'

He kissed her softly on the lips. 'I think I love you. Is that better?'

A visit to Calum's room convinced Alexander that he was faking the injury, but he could scarcely accuse him of such, when his ankle was encased in a plump bandage.

'Twisted it gettin' down from the cart,' he claimed, with a convincing wince. 'I can still get about on a walkin' stick, but it looks like I'll need your help over the next few days.'

Had his arrangements with Mhairi-Anne not already reached such a satisfactory stage, Alexander might well have challenged Calum, there and then. Clearly, his uncle had left strict instructions to ensure there were no 'complications' while he was away and Calum was endeavouring to comply. But he and Mhairi-Anne were both experienced adults and it was really none of their business, he concluded.

'Of course, your portrait will be delayed,' resumed Calum. 'But that can wait – these jobs can't.' He handed him a list of visits he wanted made, along with instructions.

Alexander glanced at the list. 'Don't worry. I'll start in the afternoon.'

Calum nodded smugly, while Alexander left the room, a quiet smile on his face.

Alexander's conviction that Calum's 'injury' was faked was reinforced, when he hobbled in to make a third at lunch and, subsequently, dinner. By then, Alexander was able to report some progress from his afternoon's work, however, and Calum appeared satisfied.

He had intended to stay in his room until midnight, to ensure everyone was asleep, but he could contain his impatience no longer than 11.30. Aided by a lone candle, he then made his way stealthily along the corridor. Her room was to the rear of the castle, down a narrow passage and one short flight of stairs. His heart lifted, when he found that she had left the door slightly ajar.

Sitting, still fully dressed, by her window, she was gazing out on to the moorland, which, that night, was clothed in a ghostly blue sheen by a clear starry sky. She did not rise to greet him. This was not how he had imagined the assignation countless times that day. Her apparent composure, too, was unexpected, as she turned to look at him steadily, while he felt nervous as a schoolboy on his first day in a new establishment.

'Come – sit down,' she said, when he hesitated inside her doorway.

He crossed the room swiftly now, nerves giving way to fear that she had changed her mind. This meeting felt like the beginning of an interview – not the commencement of an illicit, passionate relationship.

He sat on the edge of the seat, bracing himself for disappointment. 'You seem . . . distant,' he finally murmured, when she did not speak. 'Changed your mind?'

'About going to bed with you?' She shook her head, which reassured him somewhat, but her candour, too, was somehow incongruous and there was a deliberate quality about her whole manner which suggested a degree of rehearsal that puzzled him. He was not surprised, when she added, 'But I must explain something first.'

A strange fear gripped his heart and he laughed jerkily. 'Can't it wait?'

'I had thought it might – until . . . I realized that I could not deceive you.'

'Deceive me?' he echoed.

'I thought you were a man of the world that—'

'I was a cad?' He grimaced. 'In some ways I am . . . I have been. . . .'

'But I was being unfair . . . selfish.'

He shrugged, more than ever perplexed by her attitude. 'What are you trying to tell me?'

She clasped her hands tightly in her lap. 'I . . . we've not been honest with you. My position here is not as it seems.'

'I still don't understand.'

'I . . . I am not your uncle's "adopted daughter", Alexander,' she said slowly – quietly. 'I am . . . have been his mistress.'

A smile of disbelief formed partially on his lips, only to disintegrate at the continuing gravity of her expression. He sat back in the chair, as if winded. His eyes burned into hers, searching in vain for some indication that this was all lies – a tasteless joke. But the truth was branded there. His gaze fell away to settle dazedly on his knees. They were starting to tremble, he noticed in a detached fashion, before the rage, which was sweeping up his body, climaxed in his brain.

He shot to his feet as a deluge of humiliation, fuelled by an avalanche of recollections, hints and clues, which he had foolishly ignored or misinterpreted, flooded his mind. The random fury of his movements all around the room reflected his emotional uproar. He ended up at the door, as if about to leave, but abruptly hammered one fist violently against its panels. She looked frightened, when he then slowly turned round to lean against the door and smiled at her dangerously.

'That's why you're unpopular! Everyone knows, don't they?'

She did not respond and he demanded loudly, 'Don't they?'

'Yes – but my unpopularity began long before. . . .'

'So I was treated like an idiot,' he raged, beginning again to pace about the room. 'The only boy in the class who didn't know the teacher was sleeping with the master!' His sneering contempt erupted into a rumbling laugh. 'Oh – it's rich, so rich! On the mainland, we hide women like you in back streets out of sight of decent people.' He spread his arms widely. 'Here – my uncle parades his whore for all to recognize – except his stupid nephew, of course.'

She stood up, clasping her hands tightly in front of her. 'I think you'd better leave.'

'Oh I will – don't worry about that. What did you think to do? Swap my uncle for me, now that he's displeased you?'

'I . . . I was trying to be honest,' she muttered, a noticeable quiver now in her voice.

Alexander stopped his rampaging in front of her. 'Why didn't *he* tell me? Why did I have to be kept in the dark, when the whole island knows your dirty little secret?'

'Because he expected just this sort of ridicule and he feared you'd tell his brother. I wanted you to know from the outset.'

'You're proud of your position, I suppose?' he scoffed.

'I hate it!' she retorted with a passion which shook through her body. 'I told you once, we all have choices to make in life and I believe that. But choices are not always black or white. I have had to make decisions based on possibilities. I chose to be your uncle's mistress, as I thought I loved him, but, perhaps, I simply lacked the courage to starve.'

'You make it sound quite noble,' he said drily. 'And now you've had enough of him, you decided to try your charms on me?'

'You wanted me . . . I could have deceived you, but I didn't.'

'To avoid hurting me?' he retorted sceptically. 'How honourable! What a scheming witch you are. You knew very well that if you didn't tell me beforehand, Calum at least, would have told me later. And then I might just have become nasty!'

'You're being nasty now. I've gained nothing!'

'But you thought you'd get away with it, didn't you? Of course, I might have been a little put out at first, but a man of the world like me. . . . What's a mistress for, but to pass around a family? It's just unfortunate, I suppose, that I happen to be a little more squeamish than you envisaged, eh?'

'You've got it all worked out, haven't you?' she retorted, her face ghostly pale in the blue light streaming through her window.

'Not quite! What did you hope to get out of me, that Uncle James can no longer supply?'

She looked away from him – out of the window on to the moorland. 'I want to get away from here . . . from Neil Graham, William Morrison, everyone.' She glanced back at him. 'You may find it hard to believe, but your uncle used to say we'd marry some day. But I know now he will always put this island first. When I came here, at the beginning, he got the bargain he wanted. He and the islanders are happy, while I am reviled. This statue of your aunt is their way of signalling their contempt for me and James co-operates in it.' She looked away from him sharply, to conceal tears, he thought. But he didn't care.

'So you thought I would be your transport to another life?' he muttered icily. All the violence within him had cooled to a dull, cold ache, but he still wanted to lash out verbally, to relieve the heavy stone weight that had settled in his chest.

'Your uncle does not pay me for my services in the school – or elsewhere.'

'You believed I would?'

'I have no savings. I thought . . . I hoped you might support me for a time on the mainland – until I got a job. I was . . . desperate and I . . . I liked you. I thought you felt . . . something for me.'

'You are a calculating witch!'

'If I were, you would not be standing there now. In material terms, I have everything here that I need.'

'You were set to risk it all on me? Why?'

'I no longer love your uncle. I wanted to be free of hate.'

'Why *me*?' he demanded, agitated once more. 'But I forget. I'm probably the only male guest you've had in years!'

Her hand lashed out at his face, but he was just beyond her reach. He caught her off balance his fingers tightening around her wrist. 'Only ladies are entitled to that privilege.'

'Let me go! Get out!'

'Gladly!' He dropped her wrist and turned towards the door.

'You are right!' she called after him. 'Feelings did not matter one whit! The only requisites were "male" and "rich". That's what you think. Fine! I've had enough of your contempt.'

He did not look back and resisted the urge to bang the door loudly behind him.

In his room, he poured himself a stiff brandy – all that was left of the bottle he had stored in his luggage – and sat down by the fireside. He swallowed the liquid in two swift gulps, before he hurled the glass into the grate, where it splintered into tiny fragments, which spat and hissed in the dying flames of the fire.

CHAPTER EIGHT

MHAIRI-ANNE MacDonald was five months past her eighteenth birthday and innocent by any standards, when James McNair first made love to her. He was over forty.

She had fled her father's tyranny and another beating to seek sanctuary with Flora at Tora Castle. Flora, however, was in bed with a fever. Instead, James, the idol of her childhood, took her in, comforted her and seduced her. Since his wife had died three years before, his loneliness had been acute; by contrast to the brutal treatment of her father, his gentle hands and kisses were novel and overwhelming. For the first time in her life, she felt loved.

Raised by parents for whom bouts of violence and wars of silence were the rituals of their married life, she had found little scope for gentleness in her home. When her mother had been alive, she had tried to protect her daughter from her husband's alcoholic rages, but she had been too drained by his brutality and cruelty – both physical and psychological – as well as the unrelenting work on the croft, to offer Mhairi-Anne more than a hint of the love that was locked within her, before she died. Elizabeth McNair had been kind and affectionate towards her, but it had been James who had filled all of her romantic, adolescent dreams. For her, their lovemaking had been the fulfilment of many innocent, wishful fantasies.

Consequently, afterwards, she experienced no regrets and she was surprised by his anxiety and distress. Naïvely, she had not thought beyond the warm contentment and security of those stolen moments. Soon, however, he shattered her illusions.

'You must know I can't marry you,' he murmured, rising from his seat beside her on the couch and beginning to pace the room. 'You're half my age – you were like a daughter to Elizabeth. I still . . . I still love Elizabeth,' he ended, distractedly running a hand through his hair, as he sat down again in a chair opposite her.

'I don't expect . . . anything,' she muttered. 'You've always been so kind. I . . . I loved Mrs McNair, too. I'm sorry – I know we shouldn't have. . . .'

'It wasn't your fault. Don't think I'm blaming you, but the thing is – you can't stay here again – not after this.'

'But . . . but where will I go? My father. . . .' Terror and alarm left her momentarily with no pride, but she stopped before she humiliated herself further and stood up. 'Of course, I'll go . . . I—'

'I don't mean right now – not tonight!' He stood up beside her, pressing her back into the couch, where he, too, sat down again. 'But tomorrow – we must find you somewhere else to live – somewhere safe – so that you won't need to come here any more.'

Growing hurt and shame now kept her silent. She had stayed many nights at the castle in the room next to Flora to escape her father's brutality, and could not yet grasp the enormity of the change in their relationship, which meant this could not continue. Eventually, a possible explanation crept into her mind. 'Are you afraid I might be pregnant?' she asked hesitantly, her cheeks glowing.

He shook his head on a sigh. 'That's not possible. Why do you think Elizabeth and I never had children? It wasn't *her* fault. What I mean is – you don't need to worry about that.' He hesitated – this revelation embarrassing enough – but he had to say more. 'The thing is – if you keep coming here, it could happen again – people could start to talk. The islanders already think you've been favoured, but they saw that as Elizabeth's doing. As proprietor, I need their co-operation and respect – for the good of everyone.'

'I . . . I understand,' she murmured, her hurt giving way to the slowly dawning realization that the hero of her childhood was that no more. In his own way, he was as afraid as she was. The thought disturbed and alienated her and she stood up once more. 'I'll go upstairs.'

He rose beside her. 'Tomorrow – we'll find somewhere safe for you, I promise.'

'My father will be sober tomorrow. I'll go home again. I always do.' Her firmly clipped words, belied the lump gathering force at the back of her throat.

He lifted one hand to her cheek. 'I'm sorry . . . so sorry.'

She jerked a smile and hurried from the room, before tears overcame her. Often – later – over the years since that fateful liaison – she had wondered if she had ever really loved him again after his rejection that night – or if she had ever really loved him, in the first place.

The following day, she left the castle before dawn. Hurt, embarrassment, shame and pride collaborated to send her running and slipping over the dewy moorland to her croft, before there was any danger of James being up to see her leave. When she reached home, she stood outside, listening to her father's rhythmic snoring, as she watched the morning sky slowly lightening, and it was then that she came to a decision. Last week, she had turned down Neil Graham's proposal of marriage. She did not love him – or so she had thought. But what did she know of love – nothing – after last night. She had worshipped James McNair, but he had fallen like a heathen idol, with the revelation of his fallibility: his reputation meant more than any feelings he had for her. Was love any more reliable? Had her mother ever loved the creature who had driven her to her grave? Neil Graham was sober – honest – hardworking, like his father. She might grow to love him. He said he loved her. She would show James McNair that she needed his help no more!

Three weeks later, she married Neil Graham in Tora church. When she had gone to him to indicate her change of mind, he had been ecstatic, even when she had told him very plainly that she did not love him, as he loved her.

'Love will come,' he had assured her. 'Love is growin' and livin' together. You need me – that's just as important. I understand you wantin' to get away from your father. That's no life for you.'

James McNair's name, of course, had never been mentioned and although some tongues had wagged on Tora regarding the apparent haste of their union and Mhairi-Anne's slim figure had been scrutinized carefully by every matron on the island, their wedding plans had gone ahead without a hitch.

Neil Graham, senior, was a highly respected figure and his eldest son basked in his reflected glory. Tall, broad and muscular, he was seven years older than Mhairi-Anne – the most eligible bachelor on the island – as she was often told, since the Grahams were considered better off than most folk, with their five strapping sons all able to contribute to the family income. Physically, he was certainly handsome enough to attract the eye, Mhairi-Anne thought, with dark curly hair like his father and deep-set brown eyes, and he treated her with a kind of reverence and respect, which should have delighted her, considering the brutality of her father's treatment. But as she got to know him better over the weeks before their marriage, she became even more acutely aware of the spiritual gulf between them, that had little to do with their differing views on religion. Her mainland education had bred in her a love of reading, music and art, which they could never share and she realized even then that her thoughts on many issues would always be her own. This lonely awareness and her spiralling certainty that she could never love him constituted an aching void within her, but nobody could have guessed at her unhappiness on her wedding day. Already she was growing skilled in concealing her feelings – an attribute she honed to perfection over ensuing years.

Representatives from nearly every family on the island attended the ceremony in Tora church, so much so that the doors remained open and half the congregation lined up outside, to see Neil Graham, senior, give away the smiling bride – a plan hatched in the certain knowledge that Mhairi-Anne's father could not be relied upon to remain sober, even for one day. Celebrations then centred on the Graham family's croft, with tables set outside in the fine weather that prevailed and pigs roasted on spits to feed the gathering of guests – among them, Mhairi-Anne, noticed – none other than James McNair.

She had not seen him since that night three weeks before and her cheeks burned, as he came forward in the wake of other guests, to congratulate them both on their marriage. Forced to look him in the eye, as he held her hand briefly, she saw only relief in his expression. Evidently, she had done the right thing, as far as he was concerned, and she told herself this should not annoy her, but it did.

'Your father didn't make it, I see,' he said to her briefly, while Neil shook hands with people following on.

She shook her head. 'I didn't expect he would. In fact, I didn't want him here!' Her eyes met his in a moment of defiance, which she hoped communicated that these feelings applied equally to him.

When he left shortly afterwards, with nothing more than a wave, a cold determination settled in her stomach. She would make her marriage work – she had to. There was no escape now, even if she wanted it.

Their first night together was spent in the new croft, which had been hurriedly erected since the announcement of their wedding plans. It was barely a mile away over the moorland track and, as the sun began to cast an orange haze over the sea, they walked there together, hand in hand – the calls, the laughter, the good wishes of the islanders, echoing in their wake.

For most of the way, Mhairi-Anne was silently apprehensive, while Neil talked spasmodically about his plans for their croft.

He stopped with an embarrassed laugh, when he realized that he had gone so far as to imply that they had children running around and it occurred to her that he was as nervous as she was about the night ahead. Although her experience with James had taught her what she might expect, her essentially passive role in that liaison had left her none the wiser about how she should behave now. Over past weeks, they had kissed – no more. For all she knew, it could be his first time. She longed to ask, but did not dare.

Inside the croft, he lit the lamp, before turning again to the door.

'I'll wait outside – have a smoke – while you get ready.'

She nodded mutely, before he closed the door quietly behind him, leaving her alone. As she gazed around the tiny room, filled with all the practical paraphernalia of crofting life, the full enormity of what she had chosen to do, suddenly enveloped her, like the shadows dancing eerily all around, cast by the flames of the fire. With her father, she had regularly known fear and loneliness, but there had always been dreams of escape. Now they, too, were gone. Nothing had prepared her for the crushing sense of spiritual isolation, which wholly enclosed her. There was no way back. She had walked into a trap of her own making. And for several minutes she simply stood there – paralysed by the yawning, awful certainty, that she had made a dreadful, irrevocable mistake.

When, finally, she moved to undress, she found her face was wet with tears she'd never shed. A kind of panic took over. Buttons would not open. Strange noises escaped unbidden from her lips, as she frantically ripped at her clothing and watched the door, like an animal awaiting execution. By the time she had donned her white nightdress, her hair hung in a loose tangle over her shoulders and none of her fingers would work to braid it. As the door opened, she leapt into the set-in box-bed, drawing the covers high under her chin.

She never knew whether it was Neil's first time or not. The

initial gentleness of his approaches rapidly gave way to a desperate, fumbling clumsiness, when her body remained utterly unresponsive to his touch. The urge to cry out and fight him was so powerful within her, that it was all she could do to stop herself resisting. At the final invasion, her nails drew blood on his shoulders, but it was he who cried out, not she. She feared if once she lost control, she would never stop screaming. Some part of her felt she deserved this. She had married him for all the wrong reasons – to spite James McNair – to escape from her father: she had not really considered his feelings for a moment. Shortly, however, she was to discover that Neil Graham had stronger feelings than she had ever imagined and that, essentially, she had married a man she did not know in any meaningful sense at all.

CHAPTER NINE

THE physical ordeal over, they lay side by side in silence, as their breathing slowly quietened and the sounds of the crackling fire again filled the room. Mhairi-Anne longed to escape from the bed – to open the door and run over the moorland, with the wind streaming through her hair, but, trapped on the inside against the wall, she could not even move without disturbing him. He lay with his eyes closed, yet she knew instinctively he was no more asleep than she was. His body felt taut against hers; his breathing deliberate; and still he had not uttered a word. Fear held her rigid. In not fighting him, she had thought to contain her revulsion, but, perhaps, he knew; perhaps, he had hated it as much as she had; perhaps, he, too, was realizing what a terrible mistake he had made.

'Who was he?' His voice was startling after the long quiet and his eyes opened slowly like one rising from the dead.

'What . . . what . . . ? I don't understand.'

'Who was he that had you before me?'

'I . . . I . . . don't understand . . . what you're talking about.' Terror had risen like vomit in her throat. How could he know? How could she ever tell him? James McNair! All hell would break loose – the Grahams might lose their croft – James would be a laughing stock.

He rolled over on to his side, his dark eyes glaring at her. 'Tell me who it was!'

'Nobody . . . there was nobody.'

'You're a liar!' His fingers bit painfully into her shoulder blade, so that she cried out.

'Neil – please – believe me! There's been no one . . . no one.'

He thrust her away from him. 'I'll find out – Tora isn't big enough to hide him. I'll find out.'

'Neil, why are you doing this? I'm *your* wife – *yours*! I married *you*!'

'Aye – an' why was that, I'm askin' myself now? One week, it's "Naw" – then it's "Aye" – and you were brazen enough to tell me you didn't love me.'

'I was honest, Neil! And you said that didn't matter – that love would grow, but how can it, if you treat me like this?'

'Honest?' he echoed contemptuously. 'About what?'

'About . . . everything!' she insisted desperately. 'Why do you think there's been someone else?'

'Men know these things. Virgins bleed. I can tell just by lookin' at you now.'

She shook her head despairingly. 'It's not true . . . not true.'

'I *loved* you!' he declared brokenly. 'I had you up here on a pedestal – above them all!' He thrust one of his hands in the air – gesticulating wildly – before bringing it down on her hair. Involuntarily, she stiffened, shrinking away from him, as his fingers stroked the long tresses which spilled over the blankets. Her revulsion infuriated him further. 'Now look at you!' he cried, winding her hair round his hand and pulling her roughly towards him. 'I want to know who made you into a tart!'

'You're hurting me!' she hissed at him, fear finally giving way to anger. 'Let me go!'

Instead he drew her closer to him. 'You're my wife – remember! And this is our weddin' night.'

'No!'

His mouth smothered her scream.

This time, she fought him, but to no avail. Ironically, when it was over, it was Neil, who cried like a baby, not her. Lying mutely beside him – she listened – blaming herself. She had had no idea that he might suspect her past. Sex education had not been on her school curriculum and her mother had never discussed it with her. He knew no other way to love her and she had taken that love and dishonoured it with her lies. Even as she hated him she pitied him, too. He had been raised in the strict Torean belief in the chastity of 'decent' women, the sanctity of marriage and the purity of love. Anything else was beyond his understanding. While he had readily accepted her admission that she did not love him, the idea of her defiling the body that he had promised to cherish was intolerable. He had opened his Christmas present and found it broken. And she realized already that he would not rest until he discovered the identity of the culprit.

A week later, an ironic twist that underlined the mistaken nature of their union came with the news that her father had been found dead on the moors. In a drunken stupor, he had evidently fallen and frozen to death, after lying out all night. They buried him without a tear being shed. Mhairi-Anne had cried herself dry since her wedding night, and had nothing left to bemoan the passing of a man, who had, arguably, precipitated the current tragedy, which was dogging her, as well as countless others. Neil, she noticed, was gentler with her over the days of the wake. But understanding was something else. Her apparent lack of grief, even at the grave-side, was another strange phenomenon in her character which disturbed him. Could it have been her father, he wondered? Later, he asked her. Her hysterical reaction provoked another scene. She had actually laughed at him.

'You're mad! Mad!' she screamed. 'My father was never sober long enough!'

He had slapped her for that. It was not only that she had shown him her 'vulgar' side – it was her crushing of another hope. He might have forgiven her for that – knowing what MacDonald was like – but she had not begun to appreciate the ridiculous irony that incest might have provided her with her only way out.

Even the frail hope that Neil might soon be thwarted in his quest for 'the man', if he chose to keep the calamitous nature of their union private, proved futile over ensuing weeks. Gradually, the obsession escaped beyond the bounds of his pride and his control. Firstly, his father realized something was amiss, and eventually Neil told him. And *he* confronted Mhairi-Anne.

'It's none of your business,' she told him angrily. The jealous mania feeding her husband's increasing brutality was hardening her.

'It's my business when I see my son demented by the likes of you,' Graham retorted. 'How could you do this to him? How could you reduce him to this? He can't think straight – he can't work. Tell us who it was and be done with it.'

She was, by now, beyond denials. 'And what would that achieve? Will he feel better if he can beat him up – throw him into the sea?'

'So – you don't deny it then?'

'I've denied it till I'm blue in the face! He doesn't believe me. You don't believe me. All I'm saying now is I'd give a name – any name, to be done with it. But what good would that do?'

'It would give him back his pride!'

'If he murdered someone?'

'The jealousy's murderin' *him*! You've got to tell him.'

'I can't help you – or Neil,' she muttered wearily.

'Then God help you Mhairi-Anne MacDonald! 'Cause you'll need it, before anyone on this island forgives you for this.'

By the time they had been married three months, their 'secret' was all over Tora and she realized wretchedly that even James McNair must have heard the gossip about them. Common sense told her that he could not possibly visit her; yet daily, she somehow expected him. Everywhere she went, people whispered in her wake. Some even had the effrontery to call out obscenities behind her back and she grew courageous in turning round and facing them with all the defiance she could muster. And the more brazen she apparently became, the more sympathy her husband attracted. He grew the heroism of a man greatly wronged by a deceitful witch, who might have turned anyone's head. Hadn't young Robert McKay fallen off the cliffs at Tora Point, while under her thrall?

The miserable realization that she was actually pregnant almost broke her spirit completely. She stopped going out and spent her days working like a fiend on the croft, while she contemplated a myriad of ways to commit suicide. Leaping from Tora Point into the pulverizing force of the rocks below became obsessive viewing in her mind. She felt she was going mad. Sometimes she seemed to fly through the air in her mental images, before everything became an exploding black; other times she fell, hitting every rock on the way and splattering the images gory red; and, occasionally, the sea took her far away and she awakened choking and drowning in a nightmare.

It was through her nightmarish visions that Neil became aware that she was going to have a child. She had not even considered telling him – knowing very well that he would only see this development as confirmation of her promiscuity – but when she awakened one night in a sweat, clutching her stomach and delirious, he guessed, and, as anticipated, the possibility that it was his child, did not figure in his reaction. He shrank from her, as if she were poison, and began hurriedly putting on his clothes.

'Where are you going?' she asked. 'Neil – it's your baby – yours! I swear!'

He did not respond until he was fully dressed. Then he leant over the bed and hissed in her face, 'I'm goin' to get drunk – drunk – so I can forget I've ever known you.'

He left the croft, banging the door behind him and that was the last time she ever saw him. When he did not return the next morning, she concluded he must have gone to sea, as usual, with the fishing fleet and she fretted all day – wondering what he would do on his return. But it was Neil Graham, senior, who eventually appeared at the croft, late that night, with the news that Neil had been lost at sea along with another member of the crew. She was stunned.

'Sit down! Sit down!' she implored, as the man looked at her through a haze of grief, but he remained standing in her doorway, inconsolable.

'You did this! You and your bastard!'

She backed away from him, expecting him to strike her, but, instead, he turned and strode off, leaving her door, flapping in the wind.

As the bodies were never recovered, there was a memorial service in Tora church a week later. Mhairi-Anne did not attend – only learning of this much later. No one came near the croft during this time and she dwelled in a strange state of limbo – one moment fearing for her life – the next, wishing someone would end it.

When she awakened from another nightmare, she thought at first her visions had taken on a new dimension of hell. Flames were everywhere; smoke smarted in her throat and nostrils; and the bedclothes were smouldering at her feet. But it was no nightmare! The croft was a blazing inferno around her.

How she penetrated the walls of flames, she never could remember. James McNair found her the following morning, lying in a frozen heap on the moorland slope beside the smouldering croft. Nothing was left to salvage. The fire had taken everything and almost her life.

CHAPTER TEN

THREE days later, Mhairi-Anne surfaced from unconsciousness and found herself in a spacious bedroom at Tora Castle. At her bedside sat James McNair, apparently asleep, but her movement instantly awakened him. As she looked dazedly across at him, he grasped her hands in his. 'You're going to be fine. Everything's going to be all right.'

She tried to speak, but no words would come. Her throat felt as if it was on fire. 'It's the smoke. Don't try to talk,' he said gently. 'You don't need to worry about anything. From now on, you'll stay here.'

She shook her head helplessly on the pillow and he gripped her hands more tightly.

'I'm sorting everything out. You wait and see. They've gone too far. I'm the owner of this island and I'll decide what happens from now on.'

Tears of grief and frustration spilled over her eyes and he sat on the edge of the bed to wipe them away gently before he continued softly, 'I love you Mhairi-Anne. I've been through hell with you, but you never knew it. When you married Graham, I could have killed him that day, but I realized it too late. And when I heard all the . . . rumours . . . I wanted to come to you, but I was . . . afraid. Afraid! I told myself I would only make matters worse, but I was a miserable coward. Please, forgive me!'

Moving her hands in his was the only response she could make. Although she could not speak, she felt as if she had died in Hell and awakened in Heaven. Was it possible the agony was over? He raised her fingers to his lips and kissed them before he resumed, 'I've spoken to Graham. He knows now – about us – but he did not dare accuse me. They'd overstepped the mark, you see, him and his sons. He knows I could have them arrested for arson and attempted murder. There were witnesses and some of them would talk, if I put pressure on them. The Grahams will leave you alone now – or they'll go to gaol. If it wasn't for the fact that I'd have a revolt on the island, I'd put them behind bars now.'

Mhairi-Anne again pressed his hand and he bent and kissed her cheek. Their faces close, he whispered, 'One day, we might be married – when things settle – people will come to accept you.'

She could only look at him in wonder. Was any of this possible? Could she know peace again? Did she want to marry James McNair – or any other man again? Her mind had no answers to these questions. She felt as if she had been reincarnated in another life and was yet an infant, without any ideas of her own, so that decisions were being made for her. This thought prompted her to force two barely recognizable words out of her constricted throat.

'The . . . baby?'

He kissed her again. 'It's gone,' he said softly. 'It was for the best.'

She cried then – hoarse choking sobs racking her body, and for a time she was inconsolable, yet she did not comprehend the reason for her grief. God only knew she had never wanted the child that had taken root in her body. But, perhaps, this was reason enough.

Within a week, she was able to get up from her bed, and within two weeks, she had realized how dramatically her life had altered yet again. There was no more grinding labour on the croft, no more living with fear as a companion at the dinner-table each evening – and no more fighting blindly in the dark. Her days took on the comparative luxury of castle life; John and Flora, who had known her since childhood and whose loyalties lay firmly with James, were kind and waited on her; she could read, sew tapestries, play the grand piano in the library and, best of all, she could sketch and paint again – and she had James as her companion, her intellectual equal, on a level to which Neil Graham could never have aspired.

The future, too, looked bright. James had decided to reopen the old schoolhouse, which had been closed for two months, for want of a teacher, and he had promised the post would be hers and she would have pupils. The whole experience had evidently given him a new appreciation of his power on the island. Before, he had lived in Elizabeth's shadow – too aware that Tora had first been hers. But *he* was owner now and it was as if he had suddenly realized what this entailed. Crofters were issued with new annual leases, containing the condition that their children attend the local school. He wanted an educated workforce on Tora and he would have it, he told Mhairi-Anne determinedly.

She should have been happy, she told herself many times, and she might have been, but for two features of her new life-style. One visit to Castlebay village was enough to demonstrate that in the world outside the castle, nothing had really altered for her. Although no one now dared to shout vulgarities at her in the street, the continuing hate and silent contempt of the islanders was almost a tangible force, wherever she went. That her lover had turned out to be none other than their lord and master, had been a bitter pill for them to swallow, but there were many reasons why *he* could be exempted from their scorn. Men would have their fun, after all, and James McNair was a man who had the power to evict them from their crofts, if they did not tolerate his *weakness*. But *she* was a different matter. Certainly some thought Neil Graham had gone too far in almost burning her alive, but they could understand and sympathize with the feelings that had prompted his uncharacteristic behaviour. It was all *her* fault really: *she* drove men out of their heads. Even her father could be excused his drinking now, with such a witch as his daughter! In a way, they could feel sorry for James McNair, too, because she would bring him no luck.

That Mhairi-Anne soon realized all of this and discussed it with James altered nothing. He could force compliance on a practical level, but he was not a god. He could not alter hearts and minds and he urged her to be patient. Only time could change such perceptions, he insisted. But time, she discovered over the years, had a way of standing still on Tora – at least with regard to her.

The second issue that marred her new life at the castle was on a more personal level. As soon as she was physically well again, James blithely assumed that she would wish, as he evidently did, to resume their affair, and, at that time, fresh from the fearful tragedy of her marriage, she could not find the courage to reject him. His earlier behaviour had to be forgiven, in light of all he had done for her since; he said he loved her and she was fond of him; she also knew with dark certainty that she was destined to a lonely life on Tora if she turned her back on him. It seemed in every way senseless, therefore, to risk offending him and causing unhappiness – all because she could feel no physical pleasure in their relationship. And so the pattern was set. . . .

When Calum came to stay at the castle, there was little need to explain anything and, if James did, Mhairi-Anne never knew about it. Calum was liked all over the island and, indeed, remembered by some from his youth. Mhairi-Anne had no doubt that he would very soon learn all the details of her story and she half expected his respectful attitude to alter, at some point, when he discovered her infamy. But from the start, he seemed to like her and that never changed – regardless of anything he learned.

The scheme that James finally hatched to attract his errant nephew and heir to Tora scarcely interested her at all. She had no desire to meet this idle rogue, as she had come to regard him, and the fact that James had finally to stoop to subterfuge to get him to the island, did nothing to commend him. Furthermore, James's insistence that Alexander must never know of their relationship was a deception she did not relish. It was another mark of her degradation, which, increasingly, she had come to resent, with the persistent attempts of the islanders to raise Elizabeth McNair's name to sainthood.

Thus, when finally she came face to face with Alexander McNair, Mhairi-Anne had been totally unprepared for the shocking force of the physical attraction he provoked in her, and even less ready to deal with the slowly dawning realization that she was falling hopelessly in love with him. She had spent years learning how to sublimate her feelings to suit those around her; to deny yearnings for something she could scarcely even imagine; to reconcile herself to the idea that the kind of love expressed in poetry and literature did not really exist. But in his company, she found she came wickedly and wonderfully alive inside, and it took all of the skills she had painfully acquired over the years, to camouflage the fact that she wanted him, evidently as much and more than he wanted her. Because – in all her private moments – she knew and relentlessly told herself that what she wanted was impossible.

The fact that the ongoing conflict over Elizabeth's statue developed to a climax during his stay, she recognized instantly as a dangerous coincidence. Suddenly she started to contemplate the impossible and to justify it. James had no intention of marrying her; surely she deserved some happiness – however fleeting; for once in her life, could she not simply please herself what she did? Such feelings had informed her momentary defiance in kissing Alexander that night in the darkened hallway, but she had stopped in time. The next morning, James had apologized. They would sort this all out, he had promised, once Alexander left the island and she had realized anew that what she wanted was utter madness. If she succumbed to his pagan appeal, she would be left behind, more miserable than ever. And that was the very least of the possible consequences. If James found out, her infidelity would be unforgivable.

When James left for Inverness, however, taking her painting of Elizabeth with him, without further discussing the issue with her, all reason and resolve seemed to go too. It was all too easy to exaggerate her feelings of anger and betrayal in the interests of allowing freedom to desires that were crying for escape. The impossible . . . the unthinkable . . . assumed the attractive guise of irresistible opportunity. For a time, at any rate, she might know happiness she had never known before, and Alexander might help her leave the island and all its hate behind.

In this mood of rebellion, she might have rushed headlong into Alexander's arms that night, but for the intervention of Calum. While Alexander was out doing the list of jobs he had concocted for him, he sent for her.

'What can I do for you?' she asked, on entering his bedchamber, where he sat by the fire, his supposedly injured ankle supported on a stool in front of him.

Typically, he wasted no time on small talk. 'You can tell me where you've put your brains to rest, for a start, lassie.'

Her face flushed, although she had been expecting something of this nature. 'It's none of your business, Calum,' she retorted, ready to leave again, now she was certain of his intention.

'Sit down,' he implored her, nodding at the seat opposite him. 'Have I ever interfered in your business before?'

She shook her head, before she settled reluctantly on the edge of the chair he had indicated.

'Well, then, I hope you'll do me the favour of listenin' for a minute, at least 'cause I can't bear to sit back and watch you and Alexander headin' for heartache – not to mention James, when he finds out what's gone on in his absence.'

For a moment, she sat gazing at her hands, before she murmured helplessly, 'I love him, Calum. It's over between James and me.'

'Does James know that?'

She shook her head. 'Not yet.'

'An' I don't suppose you've enlightened Alexander about how things have been between you an'—'

'How can I tell him?' she burst out. 'You know as well as I do that James wants him to know nothing.'

'Oh – so that's your excuse, is it? An' here I was thinkin' you know fine an' well what the lad's reaction will be, if he learns the truth.'

'Are you saying I *should* tell him?' she countered frustratedly.

'I was never in wi' James keepin' it a secret in the first place, lassie, and, if you love him, as you claim you do, you'll surely not be wantin' to start off on a lie.'

'Start off?' she echoed, her voice breaking wretchedly. 'He'll hate me, if I tell him.'

'Aye – maybe he will – but, in the end, only the truth can be forgivable.'

'You think he would forgive me?' she queried, hope momentarily lightening her expression.

Calum hated to crush that look, but nurturing false hope would do her no good in the long run. 'I didn't say that – an' that's not the only thing against you, lassie,' he responded gently. 'He comes from another world – a grand family, by all accounts, and although I think there's a lot more to him than we'd imagined, I can't see it ever being right for you an' him.' He sighed deeply, before adding almost on a whisper, 'James never married you, an' I can't see that he would do any different.'

'Do you think I don't know that?' she countered bleakly.

'So you'd settle for more of the same, would you?'

'It wouldn't be the same. I've never really loved James – the way I love him.' She paused, before murmuring, 'I shouldn't be saying all this to you . . . I. . . .'

'But you're right in sayin' it wouldn't be the same, I suppose, though maybe not for the reasons you're thinkin'. He's young, lassie. His folks will be expectin' him to settle down one day – with a wife – an' a family. Have you thought what that could mean?'

She looked at him – her startled expression telling him that her deliberations had never taken her that far. With James, she had always been the only woman – his 'wife' in that sense. With Alexander, she would not even have that security. She could end up the other woman. How could she bear even the possibility of it?

The thought shot her to her feet and she moved across to Calum's window, pretending to look out, as she concealed the turmoil of emotions washing over her face. Her back to him, she said shakily, 'I've . . . I've been an utter fool, haven't I?'

He rose and went over beside her, to place one hand comfortingly on her shoulder. Tears spilled from her eyes, as she turned to him, head down, wiping her cheeks with her fingers. 'Here!' He handed her a rough handkerchief from his pocket.

She blew her nose and managed to look up at him with a glint of a smile. 'I see your leg's better.'

'Aye, well, we heal quick in these parts,' he retorted, before adding softly, 'What will you do?'

'Tell him! That will be an end to it.'

'An' James?'

'That's over, too, Calum. One thing I've learned out of this mess: I can't go on as we were any more.'

Calum nodded thoughtfully, before his eyes caught sight of Alexander, galloping back to the castle over the moorland slope. 'He was quick,' he murmured, jerking his head towards the window.

She glanced down to see Alexander cantering into the castle courtyard and her heart swelled, as always, at the sight of him. Determinedly, she looked away, as her eyes misted over again. 'He'll hate me,' she murmured brokenly.

'An' what happens, if he doesn't?' queried Calum, as she gazed down at the handkerchief, held like a bouquet in her hands.

'I'll get this washed for you,' she responded, before looking up with a manufactured smile, as she added bitterly, 'Don't worry, Calum. I love him, but he only thinks he loves me.'

*

After Alexander left her room that night, she remembered her words to Calum. How right she had been! The cruel predictability of his reaction had left her in a desolation beyond tears. As she mechanically undressed and lay down in her bed, she did not allow herself to dwell on the fragile hope she had cherished that – against all reason – he might behave differently. By comparison, it would be easy to face James on his return, she thought instead, as she lay staring, glassy-eyed, at the ceiling above her bed. She seemed to watch, unseeing, while its ghostly blue sheen darkened and vanished, as the night lengthened and clouds moved stealthily in from the sea, with a rising wind that whistled mournfully over the moorland, in tune with the aching loneliness of her heart.

CHAPTER ELEVEN

AFTER returning to his room, Alexander lay fully clothed on his bed, listening to the regular chimes of the grandfather clock in the hall, until he had counted three. The alcohol had not soothed him. On the contrary, his whole body longed for action, while his mind longed to rest.

An unrelenting merry-go-round of images, thoughts and words revolved in his brain, like a jigsaw thrown angrily in the air and irrevocably jumbled. His feelings vaulted between despair and rage, as, amidst all, he knew for certain only one thing: he still wanted her! The knowledge tortured him so that he hated himself – hated the insensible puppet of craving he had become – while she could sit calmly and reveal the indecency of her life. It was not to be borne!

As another wave of fury engulfed him, a question stormed into his tortured head and he latched on to it, like a lifeline thrown to a drowning man. Why shouldn't he have her? She had not changed her mind, she had changed the rules. He could pay her, he thought suddenly! Slowly, he sat up in bed. She had been kept by his uncle for years. Money could buy his freedom from this terrible lust. The fact that he had never needed to pay a woman for sex in his life was irrelevant. He had never been obsessed by a slut before, and she was a slut like no other. This must be the way – the only way – to rid her poisonous attraction from his blood. Once he had possessed her, it would surely be over.

He moved quickly, as the resolution took hold of him and found in his luggage a purse containing twenty new guineas, which he jammed into his pocket. His emergency fund, he called it! To her, it would represent a small fortune: to him it was a route back to sanity – cheap at the price. The action exhilarated him. He could end it all tonight; cleanse himself of her devilish influence – and buy sweet revenge for his uncle's duplicity.

The clock chimed the half-hour once more, as he stole again along the corridor to her room. He held his breath for a long moment when he thought the door was locked, but with only a little pressure from his knee, it jarred open. She was in bed, but evidently not asleep, as her head turned instantly on her pillow. Their eyes locked in a soundless telepathy of intention, while he shrugged off his braces and his trousers.

The sheets felt cool against the heat of his skin and the thick tresses of her loosened hair flowed silkily across the pillows. When he moved his nakedness against her, he felt her sharp intake of breath and he buried his lips in the luxurious softness of her neck, until she was groaning softly in his ear.

Now the moment had come, there was no rush. This was the antidote to his obsession: the vessel into which he must plunge himself, or go mad. But she could not escape him now. This thrill must last forever. He unlaced the front of her nightgown with tantalizing slowness, tasting every inch of the smooth skin he exposed – not satisfied until she was breathing and perspiring as laboriously as he was. As he slipped her nightgown from her shoulders, he pinned her arms to her sides, revelling in the firmness of her breasts, while she trembled gloriously beneath him. When finally she writhed free of her gown and lay naked before him, for a moment, he was paralysed by her pagan beauty, as his eyes slid reverently over every slender inch of her flesh.

One move against the curving softness of her body now and the control, which he had exercised so skilfully thus far, was lost. There was but one thought – one agonizing compulsion: to unite his flesh with hers; to savour the diabolical climax, before it rushed too swiftly to claim him. The moment was ferocious in its intensity. The shivering shockwaves that rent both of them were accompanied by a moaning eruption of pleasure: a pinnacle of sensation that left them gradually exhausted and falling steeply into awareness.

He lay for a time, her head cradled on his chest, her hair a blanket across his slowly constricting throat. She groaned when he moved away from her, turning in a dazed heap on to her back, as he dressed swiftly, an urgency to be gone before he could think, now firing his movements

He did not look at her as he tossed the purse on to the bed. Rapid strides took him to the door. In the corridor, the innocent silence of dawn greeted him and it occurred to him, as he strode to his room, that they had not spoken a single word throughout the whole episode. But he was free, he thought bitterly. He would wait on this damned island, only to confront his uncle, and have as little as possible to do with her. She had been well paid for her diabolical services. He owed her nothing.

CHAPTER TWELVE

Dawn light was flooding his room by the time that he had finished washing and he had now no desire for sleep. A glance out of the window showed that it was a fine morning and he still had much work to do for Calum. He decided to get an early start.

Seorus Dhu started from his crib in the stables, when Alexander strode in to saddle the big brown mare himself.

'Mr McNair – I'll do it – Mr McNair!' Seorus called hoarsely, struggling to his feet.

'It's all right, Seorus. I can manage,' he responded, before he threw the saddle over the animal and tightened the girth.

The mare was a spirited beast, keen on the gallop over open moorland and he drove her hard that morning, enjoying the rush of the wind in his hair and the cleansing, salty dampness of the ocean – an ever present feature of the island. He surprised two crofters at their milking time; ensured all repairs were going well; took note of some extra timber needed, before he returned at a brisk canter to the castle for breakfast.

He went first to his room to wash his hands and found, lying beside his bedside table the purse he had tossed at Mhairi-Anne the night before. The coins jingled, as he lifted it thoughtfully, passing it from hand to hand, as if it were too hot to hold. What was she playing at now, he wondered? Then he noticed the small square slip of paper, lying also on the table. Even without lifting it, he could read the bold writing: ***I am not for sale!*** There was no signature. She must be playing for higher stakes, he decided shortly. He would return the money at the first opportunity, he concluded, placing it in his inside pocket, and make it absolutely clear that he was not on the market for the long-term arrangement she was possibly seeking.

In the breakfast-room, he found Calum helping himself to a portion of scrambled eggs and Flora's delicious crusty bread. There was no sign of Mhairi-Anne.

'You must have been off early, this morning,' remarked Calum, eyeing him sideways, as he joined him at the buffet. 'Seorus said you beat me to the rise by almost twenty minutes.'

'You wanted the work done, didn't you?'

'Aye – but you're lookin' rough, if you don't mind me sayin'. Growin' a beard, are you?'

Alexander fingered the heavy dark stubble on his chin. 'Forgot to shave.'

'Aye – an' sleep as well, by the looks of you.'

Alexander helped himself to his favourite kippers, while Calum limped to the table.

'You can stop the acting, Calum,' he said bluntly, as he joined him.

'Actin'?'

'The leg! I'm not a fool. I know what you're about.'

'And what's that?'

'Keeping me out of Mhairi-Anne's clutches.'

'Ach – you're haverin', man.'

'I know all about it, Calum.'

'She told you then?'

'What an old reprobate my uncle is! As if lying to get me here wasn't bad enough. . . .'

'He didn't want you to know. That's all. He wanted you to think well of him.'

'*Well* of him?' snapped Alexander sarcastically. 'Did he hold a meeting before my arrival, to warn everyone to keep their mouths shut?'

'There was no need. The pattern's been set here for years. Most of them think too much of James to go tellin' any outsider about his goings-on – either that, or they know he'd find out soon enough who blabbed. Even Neil Graham, who hates Mhairi-Anne more than most, wouldn't risk foulin' things up between James an' you.'

'Have you any idea how it feels to be on the receiving end of such a conspiracy?'

'I can imagine. Och – I was against it from the start, as she was.'

'She's as bad as he is . . . a scheming—'

'Don't speak of her like that!'

'She's only his mistress, for God's sake!'

Calum sighed and glared at him. 'Aye, that's how the islanders see her, an' maybe that's how he sees her, too, but she's been a wife to him for nigh on nine years, in all but name only, and he's never appreciated that fact.'

'Nine years?' echoed Alexander, for the first time nonplussed. 'What age was she when this started, for heaven's sake?'

'Around eighteen, I think. She was only married to Graham about three months, or so. James and her were together long before I came back. James told me all about it one night. A bit too much to drink, he had, and it all came out. Don't go judgin' them too harshly, laddie, especially not her. She's not had much choice in the way her life's gone, as far as I can see.'

Alexander swallowed uncomfortably and laid down his fork. 'How do you mean?'

'It was Eve that tempted Adam, was it not? The Bible has a lot to answer for in these parts. Men can stray, but they'll always find a woman to blame for it. But if you ask me, she's been more sinned against. . . .' He shrugged his shoulders thoughtfully.

'I think you'd better tell me about it, Calum.'

By the time, Calum had finished the tale, Alexander had

already begun to feel shame at his conduct towards her. When his uncle had seduced her, she had been a year younger than Victoria! The night before, it had all seemed so clear – so black and white. Now, he saw the shades of grey – the difficult choices – the dilemmas that had shaped her life. But last night, he had seen what he had wanted to see – a woman he could take, without conscience, to expunge her from his heart.

He rose from the table, painfully aware of the bulging purse in his pocket. Whatever she was, she had not deserved that treatment, he realized now. He must speak to her.

The opportunity did not come that night, as expected however, and over the next two days, it was as if she had vanished from the castle. She took meals in her room and Calum relayed her excuse of a minor illness, fed to the servants, but Alexander knew that she was simply avoiding him. His wretchedness increased with every hour of her absence.

The following day, too, he was again reminded forcibly of his unprincipled conduct towards Victoria, when he had finished Calum's list and was returning to the castle through the village. The mare was trotting along past the library, just as she emerged. He knew at once that the meeting had not been contrived. She looked thoroughly taken aback to see him and reluctantly he had to stop and dismount.

'I was going to post a letter,' she explained, tapping an envelope on one arm and looking as uncomfortable as he felt. 'John told me your uncle is gone to Inverness.'

'Yes – he will be back next Thursday, I believe.' He paused, before forcing himself to make reference to that fateful Sunday. 'I've been worried about you. What happened between us – I will never forgive myself.'

Her pale cheeks coloured, but she did not flinch from his gaze. 'I'm sorry you feel such a burden of responsibility, when it was I who encouraged you.'

'I took an utterly unfair advantage—'

'Please – believe me! I do not blame you at all and it concerns me that you blame yourself.'

'You are too forgiving.'

'I am considering taking your advice and returning to the mainland.'

'Because of what happened?'

'William Morrison did not take too kindly to my refusal, and, considering all the circumstances, I feel I should remove myself.' She paused, gazing soberly around the confines of the village. 'I've realized now that one cannot run away from life – even here.'

'My advice was to go, but I don't like the idea that you're being chased from here.'

She smiled dismissively. 'I'm not running away again, if that's what you mean.' She shrugged. 'I simply don't belong here. I never did.'

Alexander digested this glumly, concluding he had a lot to answer for. This girl had obviously been through hell, since he had last seen her. It was as if she had matured ten years within the space of a few days. And to make matters worse, he had compounded this unforgivable violation, with another of, arguably, equal magnitude. The fact that Mhairi-Anne had evidently wanted him – even welcomed him – was not in doubt, but clearly, she had not deserved the vilification he had heaped on her, nor to be treated like a common whore. The thought of what he had done now chilled him to the bone.

'Do not look so grim on my behalf,' Victoria exclaimed, interrupting his thoughts with a reproving smile. 'I say again – there is nothing to forgive! How is Mhairi-Anne, by the way? I was delighted with my portrait, although she flatters me, I think.'

'She has been unwell these past two days,' he said tightly.

'But I saw her on Saturday.'

'Oh?'

'Certainly, she was paler than usual, I thought, but. . . .' She stopped, evidently measuring her words carefully. 'We were making plans – I concluded you must know.'

'Calum and I have been very busy in the wake of the storm and with work related to the summer migration of animals.'

'It's tomorrow, I believe. A lively day, by all accounts.'

'Yes, we've had little time for chat.' He paused, summoning a casual smile. 'So what have you ladies been planning?'

'I do not suppose she will mind you knowing,' said Victoria, her voice lowering, 'but, pray, do not tell your uncle, until she speaks to him. You see, he's likely to lose his teacher.'

'She's leaving the island?' he queried, trying still to maintain a casual tone.

'With me, I hope! Of course, it all depends on whether my solicitor can find a buyer for her work. She's insistent that she must be able to pay her way. At her behest, I have already deposited three of her paintings at the post office for transport to him. They await only this explanatory letter.'

As he digested this information, his expression became grave and his eyes were lost to the rolling panorama of ocean behind them.

'I thought you would be pleased to know she may be residing on the mainland with me,' she murmured, her face colouring before she added, 'Of course, she will never know about . . . what happened between us.'

His eyes darted back to her, as he comprehended her drift. 'I'm pleased you may have company,' he assured her, although he wondered what Victoria's reaction might be, if she, too, learned the truth about Mhairi-Anne's role on the island. 'But she and I have no future, I fear.'

Victoria's eyes were puzzled. 'I thought you and she may. . . .'

He forced a wide smile and shrugged dismissively. 'I have made too many mistakes on this island.'

'I hope this had nothing to do with me.'

'Not at all,' he assured her.

'You must tell her. I hope she keeps better.'

'You have not set a date to leave, as yet?'

'Arrangements are yet in their infancy. This letter also

requests my solicitor to arrange that the hunting lodge my father owned in Perth is made habitable.'

'I see.'

She tapped the letter on her arm once again. 'I must go. Goodbye, Alexander.' As she walked away without another word, he hauled himself back into the saddle, feeling more miserable than ever.

Far from wanting to be his mistress on the mainland, Mhairi-Anne was now clearly so sickened by his behaviour, as well as his uncle's, that she was rising to the challenge of gaining her independence as quickly as possible. And far from freeing himself of her, what he had done now utterly revolted him, particularly as he had realized painfully over the past two days that this extraordinary woman was not a passing obsession to be dismissed with one night of lustful satisfaction. He loved her to distraction – and against all reason.

That night, he and Calum dined once more *à deux*, with Calum doing his level best to raise his low spirits through talk of the forthcoming festivities.

'Some say the migration is the happiest day of the year,' said Calum enthusiastically. 'It's a grand outin' for the whole island and the youngsters and old dears love stayin' on at the *shielings* to take care of the beasts.'

'*Shielings*?'

'Their temporary summer homes – makeshift dwellings, they may be, but the views make up for the leakin' roofs and the nippy nights. For young and old, it's a grand get-together. Makes up for all the lonely winter nights.'

'When will they return?'

'The young ones come back each weekend for provisions, but it'll be the end of July, before we all go out again one evenin', to feast and ceilidh all night and then face the homeward trek in the mornin'.'

Alexander smiled faintly. 'I guess there will be a few sore heads on that trudge.'

'Aye,' agreed Calum with a grin. 'For more reasons than one. The lads and lassies will be mighty frisky by then and old eyes will be weary with the watchin' of them. There's always a quick weddin' or two in August.'

'I suppose, it will be sad in a way, too,' remarked Alexander.

'Aye, it signals the end of summer,' said Calum softly, his shrewd blue eyes examining Alexander's face. 'What's up wi' you, laddie? Are you goin' to tell me what's eatin' you, or do you want me to guess?'

'Guess!' retorted Alexander drily.

'Her upstairs.'

'Have you seen her?'

'This mornin'. And she's as tight as you are about what's gone on.'

Alexander pushed his plate away from him and sat back. 'It's all a mess, Calum. Don't ask me to explain.'

'By God, James will smell the atmosphere from this place at the harbour on Thursday. There will be hell to pay and no mistake.'

'If he had been honest from the start. . . .' muttered Alexander, his voice tailing off, as he knew he could not blame his uncle for the monumental offence he had given. He sat forward suddenly. 'I'm going up to see her. I must speak to her.'

'She's ill – in bed, Leave her be!'

Alexander stood up. 'I can't make matters any worse, Calum. Believe me.'

CHAPTER THIRTEEN

As he hurried upstairs, leaping the steps two at a time, his heart hammered against his ribs at the prospect of seeing her again, while his brain pounded with a conglomeration of ill-formed sentiments he wished to express. Much, he knew, would depend on her reaction to him.

He knocked on her door softly, but when there was no response, he turned the handle and gave the timber a push. It was locked. He knocked again more urgently.

'Who is it?' Her voice rose from within.

'Alexander.'

'Go away!'

'I want to speak to you.'

'Go away!' she repeated, her voice raised determinedly.

'You'll have to come out of there sometime and, if you don't see me now, you'll find me sitting here.'

She evidently approached the door at this. Faintly, he could now hear her breathing. 'I don't want to see you. I don't want to speak to you. *Please* – go away!'

'I'm staying!' he retorted, promptly sitting down on the floor, his back to the wall opposite her door.

Silence reigned for several minutes, before he shifted his position, deliberately to advertise his continuing presence. Still, he stared at the closed door. Another minute passed. Finally, the key turned.

He sat where he was, not wishing to frighten her now by

rushing his entrance. She took one glance at him sitting resignedly on the floor, before returning once more into her room. He rose and followed, closing the door softly after him, by which time she stood by the window, as far away from him as possible.

'Stay where you are,' she ordered, when he made to move closer. He shrugged and leaned back against the door. 'I've no intention of touching you.'

'What do you want?'

He struggled now to find appropriate words and she turned her back on him, to gaze out of her window.

'Well?' she prodded.

'I want to ask your forgiveness.'

She whirled round. 'For making love to me, or treating me like a whore?'

'I was going out of my mind with jealousy . . . rage . . . I wanted you. I thought that was the only way.'

She nodded contemptuously. 'What you want, you buy. It must be wonderful to have such power.'

'On the contrary, I feel powerless against my feelings for you. Why else, am I here? I am deeply ashamed of what I did.'

'Ashamed you made love to me?' she countered, her voice low.

'That I thought you were for sale – damn it! I'll . . . I'll never regret the other.'

Her eyes flickered unsteadily under his searing gaze and she looked evasively out of the window again.

'Calum has told me something of your life,' he resumed in the silence. 'I realize now I had no right to judge you, as I did.' He paused, as she still looked away from him. 'I suppose it was easier for me to see you like that, because then I thought I could forget you.'

She glanced round for the first time, seeming to relent. 'Sit down, if you want.' She gestured towards the chair opposite the one in which she now sat down.

At this proximity, a wave of recollections of their intimacy engulfed him and he could tell she felt similarly affected. She looked pale, but more beautiful than ever, he thought, with her hair in one thick plait, which lay over her shoulder. The deep crimson of her casual gown contrasted with her pallor and leant her flawless skin a translucent quality, while her eyes, troubled as they were, revealed a vulnerability he had never noticed before.

Eventually, she murmured, 'What I told you must have been a shock, but when you returned. . . .' She shrugged her slim shoulders. 'I wanted to believe that you understood.'

'I'm still struggling to understand,' he confessed. 'That night you spoke of going to the mainland and of needing support. I suppose that's partly why I resorted to money.'

'Partly?'

'After all you told me, I could not then believe I still wanted you. The money made my feelings acceptable somehow – justified my behaviour.' He paused before adding, 'It was more about the way I felt, than about you. And then you did not resist me. . . .'

'More than that,' she conceded softly, looking down at her hands. 'The truth is I was attracted to you from the first. It is over between James and me, although he does not know it yet.'

'Because of what he did with the portrait?'

She shook her head. 'Our relationship was dying before you came here. You made me realize – oh – so many things. I think we all do things in life that have hidden motives we do not care to recognize at the time. I told myself I could hurt him through you when, in fact, against all common sense, I . . . I. . . .' She suddenly spread her hands in a gesture of bewilderment.

He moved swiftly, catching them in his own and pressing them to his lips. 'I love you!' he muttered hoarsely.

'It's impossible. We can only be hurt. The other night, I spoke of practicalities on the mainland, as I know I cannot hope for more, but even that was a dream, Alexander. You said it yourself.

I'd have to be hidden away and one day you would want to marry some decent—'

'Never!'

'You are too young to settle for me. You will want children . . . respectability.' She dragged her hands from his and stood up, moving away.

He followed, restraining her, gathering her tightly in his arms. 'On the mainland, no one will know you. We could be married. Who is to say no?'

'And what of Tora? One day all this will be yours?'

'Perhaps not, when my uncle finds out about us. And I don't care – nothing else matters.' His mouth found hers in a bruising kiss, which blotted out all the complications around them.

As he carried her to the bed, he murmured, 'We will find a way; we *must* find a way.'

CHAPTER FOURTEEN

THE next day, Tuesday, there was a carnival atmosphere abroad on Tora, and although none of the inmates of the castle was actually to be involved in the moving of the animals to the Mount Tora pastures, they all went to see the procession through Castlebay village, including Mhairi-Anne, at Alexander's insistence.

On one of the two mares, she looked stunning in a green velvet riding habit, her hair in a long plait and a jaunty hat perched on the front of her head. With Alexander in black riding clothes, on the bigger of the two horses, they made an arresting pair, Calum thought, as he followed with Flora, John and Seorus in the dogcart. And, no doubt, all the islanders were noticing them too, he concluded, with a resigned sigh. He had finally gone to bed the night before at eleven o clock, with Alexander still in her room. He feared James would never forgive him, but he was powerless. So, he suspected, were they – against feelings that were driving them headlong to disaster.

Until his uncle returned, Alexander was determined to enjoy the time they had together and he was in a buoyant mood, after the bliss of their lovemaking.

'Seeing the light has evidently opened Seorus's eyes in more ways than one,' he teased Mhairi-Anne, as they rode along side by side. 'He was positively drooling over you back there. Perhaps he is intent on exchanging one vice for another.'

'He will require to finish the schoolhouse roof first,' she retorted jokingly.

'Is it going to be water-proof, do you think?'

'Actually, he is doing a fine job. He should finish it this afternoon.'

'I think I'll be there in case he decides to seek a reward.'

'You can help me move the desks back, if you like.'

They decided to watch the proceedings from a plateau on the moorland overlooking the village, as there was scarcely room for any more bodies in the street, with all the animals and people already there. Cows, sheep, pigs, horses, goats – many laden with equipment for the shielings – created a cacophany of noise, made all the more deafening by the din of excited islanders and a fiddler screeching out a frantic jig.

Although there was a fair wind blowing as usual, the day was fine, with only a few large clouds puffing across an otherwise blue sky. Alexander noticed a few people watching them, but, in general, everyone appeared to be too intent on having a good time, he thought, to be interested in the contingent from the castle. Dancing and singing broke out spasmodically in different areas and Neil Graham, who was evidently in charge of the march, had his work cut out creating some order in the apparent chaos of high spirits. Gradually, however, some semblance of a column emerged and, amidst choruses of gleeful shouts, the signal to move ahead was given. A fine marching Gaelic hymn immediately gathered every voice, and with smiles and waves, the migration commenced like a glorious crusade.

The procession had almost passed when Mhairi-Anne noticed Victoria standing with a group of village women.

'I must go and speak to her,' said Mhairi-Anne.

'Do not be making any more plans,' responded Alexander, as she got down. 'Our future is together, remember.'

She handed him the reins and hurried off.

He noticed that all of the women with Victoria promptly departed, as she approached, and he thought indignantly that they treated her like a leper. If he made her his wife, they would assuredly change their attitude, he thought grimly. If? That was what he desperately wanted now – to show her off to the world, without any fear of rejection, but he knew that there were dire obstacles ahead. Apart from his uncle's certain objections, his father would never approve, if he knew the truth about her, and James could certainly enlighten him, if he chose. He would be disowned; they would be penniless; and he would somehow need to earn a living for the first time in his life – a daunting prospect – but one he was prepared to face, rather than lose her. However, the problem might then be to overcome her certain rejection of such a sacrifice on his part.

As his mind filled with the maze of difficulties, that would beset any continuing relationship between them, he turned to Calum. 'I'm going to help Mhairi-Anne at the school this afternoon.'

'I want a word first.'

'Not a lecture, Calum, please.'

'On the facts of life,' retorted Calum uncompromisingly, 'in James's study.'

Alexander nodded reluctantly.

The strains of the Gaelic singing became a whisper on the wind, as the village gradually became deserted and Mhairi-Anne returned.

'How is Victoria?' he asked, as they began the journey back to the castle.

'She is full of hope for my work,' said Mhairi-Anne. 'She will be disappointed if we do not leave the island together.'

'You have not made any firm commitment?'

She shook her head. 'It is like everything else at the moment – a fantasy, I'm afraid.'

He touched her cheek reassuringly with one gloved hand.

'You are a handsome devil,' she murmured, basking in his gaze, before adding more soberly, 'I fear Victoria is in love with you as well.'

Feeling distinctly uncomfortable, he shrugged evasively. 'Did she say anything about me?'

'Just that she was happy to see you looking better than yesterday.' She paused, sensing his discomfiture. 'What's wrong?'

He swallowed on the confession that hovered on his lips. He could not risk it. 'Nothing! Come on, I'll race you to the castle,' he challenged. 'Ten of a start!'

As she galloped off, he counted slowly, every number a vicious stab of self-recrimination.

After lunch, Mhairi-Anne went ahead of him to the school, while he kept his appointment to see Calum in James's study.

'This is all very formal, Calum,' he remarked.

'Aye, well, by rights it should be James tellin' you what I've a mind to – but I thought I'd have one last try at bringin' you down to earth, before he gets back. It's about your inheritance.'

'I've already anticipated that my uncle may well change his mind, and it doesn't alter anything.'

'Oh – and here I am thinkin' you might just care a damn about the Tora folk. That was you cuddlin' Mrs Stewart on the cliff the other day, when she near lost her whole brood, wasn't it?'

'All right, Calum! No need for sarcasm, Of course, I care, but since we're discussing this anyway, you may as well know, regardless of all the complications with Mhairi-Anne, I wouldn't have financial backing, if I inherited Tora.'

'You're under orders to sell the place, or else! Is that it?'

'How did you know?'

'James knows how his brother thinks.'

'Well, that's a relief, at any rate. I wasn't supposed to tell you.'

'The fact that you let on gives me hope, but James has anticipated him cuttin' you off without a penny, if you keep the place.'

'How?'

'He's added a codicil to his will that forbids any sale of Tora in your lifetime. In short, you either keep it, or you don't have it.'

'My father will be livid about that!'

'There's always the possibility that, by the time James goes, your father won't be around to be livid about anything.'

'Then I'd be reliant on Eric's goodwill. Not a better prospect, I'm afraid.'

'According to James, Eric's had health problems, too.'

'You can't write off my whole family!' retorted Alexander.

'James hasn't written either of them out of the picture. He believes, and so do I for that matter, if faced with the prospect of keepin' Tora in the family, or not havin' it at all, a man with any sense won't turn his back. True, this island has never shown much profit so far, but who knows what the future will bring? Anythin' is better than nothin'.'

'So my father or Eric might see reason to invest in Tora to ensure its survival?'

'That's what James is bankin' on, and if they don't, you still can't sell and you'd be lookin' for someone else to invest.'

'There can't be many philanthropists like you about.'

'The point is James is set on you havin' it and providin' you don't go rubbin' his nose in the dirt over Mhairi-Anne, things will stay that way. We can't hide what's been goin' on, but if I know James, he'll come to forgive that. He's not blameless and he'll always put the good of this island first. That's why he's lost her, of course. He might have married her long ago.'

'I can't give her up, Calum! All of this could be thirty years away.'

The older man sighed. 'Or tomorrow, or next year. But you have the prospect of a happy future here. She hasn't – unless some miracle happens.'

'I've never really understood why James has always been so set on leaving the island to me, in the first place.'

'He's never been able to father a son. You're the nearest he's got to it. He talked a lot about seein' you at your brother's wedding a time back. Thought he saw somethin' of himself in you. He lost out on Strathcairn as well, you know.'

'We certainly share the same taste in women!' Alexander remarked wryly. 'But tell me – who would have the island, if he had to make good his threat?'

'It would be bequeathed to the island council for safe-keepin'. That was one of the reasons he set it up.'

'Does Neil Graham know this?'

'The whole council had to be told.'

'They probably hope I prove useless.'

Calum shook his head. 'They're not businessmen, and to prosper, Tora needs investment. They'll see you as its best hope.'

Alexander sat digesting all this information for several minutes, before he asked, 'Have you ever been in love, Calum?'

'Aye – once.'

'What happened?'

'She died – it's a long story.'

'Was there ever anybody else?'

'Not like her.'

'Then you know how I feel. Nothing else matters, compared to her.'

'Right now, nothing else matters, but look ahead, laddie, that's all I ask. I'm not only thinkin' of you; I'm fond of Mhairi-Anne, too.'

The afternoon warm, Alexander discarded his jacket in the castle and, in a pensive mood, journeyed to the schoolhouse on foot. With the sun beating down on his back, he loosened his dark waistcoat and rolled up the sleeves of his white shirt. When Mhairi-Anne saw him coming over the hill, she waved, and ran to greet him. Seorus was on the apex of the schoolhouse roof, completing the final row of slates and neither of them noticed his gaping leer, as they subsided on to sloping moorland, overlooking the school.

'We can't start until he's finished,' said Mhairi-Anne. 'The ladder's blocking the door.'

'Where are the desks?'

'In the shed.' She pointed to the low wooden structure to the rear of the main building.

Alexander now glanced up at Seorus and waved. 'How is he managing?'

'I think he had a tipple this morning at the procession. I hope he doesn't break his neck before he fits the last slate.'

Alexander laughed. 'So much for Morrison's miracle!' He lay back on the rough turf, Calum's words still ringing in his ears.

'What was the meeting all about?'

'My inheritance. It seems James is a great deal smarter than my father thought.'

'What do you mean?'

'Nothing! Lie down beside me.'

She lay back, placing her head so that it touched his, as they both looked up at the sky. The clouds of the morning had now vanished and an unblemished blue canopy enveloped them.

'I always think looking at the sky puts the world and its problems in perspective,' he murmured. 'It makes everything else seem insignificant by comparison.'

'As a child, I used to play a game of sky-gazing. If I looked hard enough, I could imagine I was anywhere else in the world.'

He turned his head towards her, touching the damp tendrils of hair which curled endearingly on to her smooth forehead. 'I wish we were anywhere else in the world.'

She sighed deeply. 'If only . . .'

He kissed the tip of her nose.

'Seorus is watching,' she murmured reprovingly.

The gathering bubble of intimacy around them was suddenly rent by an unearthly roar. Then a thud. Alexander sprang to his feet. Seorus was on the ground. As he ran, he cursed the stupidity of the man. But he had to be all right: the building was long and low; he had fallen only a few feet.

He stopped running a few yards from him. The ghastly, unnatural angle of the man's head chilled him. He walked forward steeling himself. The eyes stared up at him, wide open in frozen surprise. The mouth still gaped. A small pool of blood was growing to a grotesque halo around his head. And he knew before he touched him he was dead.

He turned instinctively to protect her from the horror of the sight, which had brought vomit to his throat, but found she had not moved from the slope. Her face was blanched; her hands were fixed to her mouth, and her eyes gazed fearfully at him, as he shook his head wordlessly.

He took off his waistcoat and placed it over Seorus's face, before he returned to her side and wrapped his arms around her. 'We'll have to get help. I think . . . he's broken his neck.'

A protesting sob broke her silence and she began to tremble violently. 'I . . . s-said i-it I . . . m-made it h-happen!' she stuttered, through shuddering breaths.

'It was an accident . . . an accident!'

'He . . . he was . . . w-watching us.' Her teeth rattled as her voice reached an hysterical screech.

'It wasn't anybody's fault!' he insisted, gripping her fiercely by the shoulders. 'It was an accident. A horrible accident!' As he shook her soundly, she quietened. Tears began to slide down her cheeks and he pressed her against his chest.

They sat thus for some minutes – the sun beating down on them – a mockery to the tragedy that had struck. Eventually, she seemed calmer and he said, 'We'll need to get help from the castle.'

She looked down at the body. 'You go. I'll stay with him.'

'No – we'll both go.'

'We can't leave him like that.'

'He's dead, Mhairi-Anne.'

'I know, but we can't leave him. Please!'

Reluctantly he rose. 'Don't go near him. Promise me, you'll just wait here.'

She nodded and he sped off.

He went straight to Calum's room when he did not locate him

in James's study, and found him dozing on his bed.

'What . . . in the name o' Satan?' Calum exclaimed, as he shook him awake violently.

'There's been an accident. Seorus fell off the schoolhouse roof.'

Rubbing his face, Calum swung his legs over the side of his bed dazedly. 'Doctor Campbell will be at Mount Tora most likely. Is he bad?'

'He'll not need a doctor.'

Calum stood up. 'What are you sayin', man?'

'He broke his neck. He's dead!'

En route to the stables, Calum asked, 'Were you inside the school when it happened?'

'No, on the slope.'

'You saw him fall?'

'No!' At the look on Calum's face, he added, 'Good Heavens! This is no time for an inquisition.'

'I'm only askin' what everyone else will ask.'

'The man's dead. It was an accident. Isn't that enough?'

'Not at the schoolhouse, when Mhairi-Anne was about.'

'Just let anyone try to blame her. . . !' Alexander threatened as he hauled the door of the stables open.

Within minutes, they were in the dogcart, approaching the scene. She was still seated where he had left her and he went to her side, while Calum examined the body. She was calm now, too calm. When Calum approached, she did not acknowledge his presence.

'She's in shock,' he opined. 'Let's get Seorus into the cart. Then we can see to her.'

Raising the body into the narrow back seat of the cart was awkward and Alexander had to take the heaviest end. As he endeavoured to gain a grip underneath Seorus's arms, the disjointed head toppled like a ball against his shirt, smearing it with blood, and he almost dropped him.

'Steady, man!' Calum shouted.

He gritted his teeth and heaved.

Finally, they had him lying on the seat and Calum covered him with a rough blanket, while Alexander, staring at the blood on his shirt, suddenly turned behind the schoolhouse to retch.

He felt Calum's hand on his shoulder.

'Here!' It was his waistcoat. 'It's clean. Cover yourself. You don't want her gettin' a close look at that.'

Alexander put on the waistcoat and buttoned it to conceal the bloodstain, before he went up the slope again and helped her down to the dogcart. 'Don't look,' he said, gently, as her eyes slid to the bundle in the back seat.

She sat quietly, cradled in his arms as they slowly returned to the castle. Calum let them off at the door.

'Get her upstairs to her room and tell Flora to see to her. And tell John to go fetch Dr Campbell and the minister. If they were at Mount Tora, they should be back by now. I'll put Seorus in the stables for now.'

Alexander was in the drawing-room, helping himself to a stiff glass of brandy, when Calum returned.

'Pour me one, as well,' said the older man, before collapsing into an armchair. 'What a day!'

Alexander handed him the brandy.

'How is she?'

'Sleeping now, I think.'

'Best thing for her,' said Calum, as Alexander, too, sat down.

'Is John away for Campbell and the minister?'

He nodded.

'I'm not looking forward to Morrison's visit.'

'Aye – well – I'd advise you to get the story straight before he arrives.'

'We were lying on the slope and he fell. That's it!'

'No – you were standin' on the slope,' corrected Calum.

'Do you really think they'll try to blame her?'

'Its a question of association, laddie! She was there when it happened.'

'So was I!'

'Aye – more's the pity, 'cause she'll be the one distractin' you from your work.'

'We couldn't move the desks because his ladder was blocking the door,' explained Alexander tightly.

'Fine – so you were just standin' talkin' on the slope waitin' for Seorus to finish, so you could get on.'

'And neither of us saw it, as we were too busy talking!' added Alexander snidely.

'Calm down, man! It'll do her no good, if you go losin' your temper in front of them.'

Alexander downed the remaining brandy in one gulp. 'I'd better get changed before they appear.'

CHAPTER FIFTEEN

THE Reverend Morrison had already arrived and was standing before the great fireplace in the drawing-room by the time Alexander returned.

'A sad day, Alexander!' he said by way of greeting. 'Most unfortunate your uncle is absent, too.'

'Yes – it's all very regrettable.'

'Calum tells me you and Mrs Graham were there when it happened.'

'Yes.'

'Conversing on the slope behind the schoolhouse?'

Alexander nodded grimly.

'Unfortunate you did not see what happened.'

'I believe he'd been drinking this morning,' said Alexander, only just recalling Mhairi-Anne's comment.

Morrison gasped a frown. 'No . . . no. That's not possible.'

'These things happen,' interrupted Calum, beginning to fidget.

'Seorus was most definitely tee-total since he *saw the light*,' continued Morrison incorrigibly.

'I doubt if you have had the time to ensure that,' retorted Alexander, barely restraining his fury at the arrogance of the man.

'It's not I who have ensured it – no, not I. Seorus has been in God's own hands over these past weeks.'

'An' God works in mysterious ways, Minister,' said Calum, coming deliberately between the two men, as he saw Alexander's eyes flash with rage. 'You've said that many a time yourself. Why don't we all sit down, gentlemen?'

Scarcely, had Morrison seated himself, however, when he resumed, 'God and the Devil, Calum. Never let us forget that God's goodness is not the only force at work among us.'

Alexander, sitting as far away from the minister as was possible in polite company, asked tartly, 'Are you suggesting the Devil had a hand in this?'

Morrison smiled thinly. 'I cannot profess to understand all of God's ways, of course. But it does seem to me that He had restored Seorus to us – sober – for a purpose that now appears thwarted by this terrible—'

'Accident!' snapped Alexander, his eyes blazing and ignoring Calum's grimace. 'But you'll excuse me.' He stood up. 'I lost my lunch earlier on and I still feel rather squeamish. I'm going for some fresh air.'

As Alexander strode from the room without further ado, Calum muttered placatingly, 'He's upset – naturally – you understand.'

Outside, Alexander sat on the low stone dyke, taking deep calming breaths. The man was an arrogant, self-righteous dolt, he thought irately. He turned when he heard feet approaching, fearing Morrison had followed him. But it was John, looking pale as milk. He had been to see the body in the stables.

'Have a seat,' said Alexander kindly. 'He's not a pretty sight, is he.'

'Flora and I will need to make him presentable for the wake,' revealed the servant, subsiding on to the wall beside him.

'I don't envy you the task. When will this be? The wake, I mean?

'Probably the two nights after your uncle gets back.'

'I've never been at such an event,' revealed Alexander.

'Ours aren't like the Irish ones,' said John, in a hushed voice.

'I understand they're quite merry affairs, with much drinkin' and a' that. There's not a drop allowed at our wakes, very sober they are, with everyone bringin' a wee gift to the bereaved household, like a pat of butter, or some tea.'

'They won't bring such gifts here, will they?' asked Alexander.

'Of course. It's a sign of respect and all the more so since it's Mr McNair's house that's been hit.'

They both turned at the sound of cartwheels, to see Dr Campbell approaching the castle and Alexander left John, as he went to greet him. To Alexander's relief, the physician's enquiries about the tragedy were discreet and to the point. Shortly he left him to examine the body and he promised to look in on Mhairi-Anne immediately afterwards.

The Reverend Morrison was still with Calum when Alexander went in, but he hurried past the closed door of the drawing-room and up to his room. The less he saw of that man, the better, he thought, as he knew Calum was right. Arguing with him would do Mhairi-Anne's reputation no good whatsoever.

Having lain down on his bed to think, emotional exhaustion overtook him. He started awake some time later. The room had darkened and a hush hung over the castle. A glance at his pocket watch told him it was now five o'clock in the afternoon. Leaping from his bed to splash water on his face, he hurried to Mhairi-Anne's room.

She was lying fully clothed on her bed, but evidently not asleep, as her head turned to greet him when he opened her door after a light knock. He kissed her gently on the lips, before he sat down on the edge of the coverlet.

'How are you feeling?'

'Better. What has been happening?'

'Morrison and Dr. Campbell have been here.'

'I saw the doctor.'

'What did he say?'

'I am to rest – that's all. How did the minister take it?'

'Spoke his usual divine nonsense,' he responded evasively, while one of her eyebrows lifted in a fashion which told him she was not fooled. But she did not pursue the subject and he drew her up, to gather her in his arms.

For several minutes, they held each other wordlessly. Eventually, she murmured, 'You must go. Calum will need your help. There will be much to arrange.'

'Dinner will be late this evening, I expect.'

'Nine o'clock, Flora said.'

'You'll be able to come down?'

'Of course.'

He kissed her once more – gently – but suddenly she clung to him, deepening the moment to a quiet breathlessness, so that his heart pounded against her chest.

'I see you are recovering,' he said huskily, before he noticed the tears on her lashes. 'What are these?' He dusted one finger softly over her eyes, glazing her cheeks.

'I'm afraid I love you too much.'

He grinned at her. 'Too little, perhaps. But never too much.'

'Go!' she ordered, smiling brightly.

He stood up, one of his hands trailing over the softness of her cheek, before he left.

By dinner-time that evening, Alexander felt ravenous and he waited impatiently for Mhairi-Anne to join them for their meal.

'Give her a call, will you?' he asked Flora. 'She might have fallen asleep again.'

'She's not in her room, Mr McNair,' Flora reported, when she returned.

'Check her studio, Flora,' said Calum. 'She's probably paintin', to take her mind off things.' He turned to Alexander. 'We best start eatin' this lot before it gets cold.'

Reluctantly, Alexander sat down and they began the meal without her.

Once more, Flora returned without Mhairi-Anne.

'She's not in her studio, or anywhere else in the castle,' said

Flora, a trace of anxiety now in her voice. 'I've had John lookin' as well.'

Alexander glanced at the window. It was now twilight; complete darkness descended with amazing rapidity on the island.

'Perhaps, she's visitin' Victoria,' opined Calum doubtfully. 'Or gone for a walk.'

Alexander shook his head and laid down his napkin. 'Something's wrong! I feel it.'

'Where are you goin'?' asked Calum.

'To have a look about outside, while there's still a glimmer of light. Flora, could you ask John to go down to the village and check if she's with Miss Liversidge?'

'I'll come with you,' offered Calum.

Over the next hour, they searched all around the vicinity of the castle, Alexander becoming increasingly anxious. There was no trace of her anywhere. When John returned with the news that she was not with Victoria, they covered every room in the castle, in a vain hope that she had, perhaps, been taken ill somewhere. But no sign! Outside, the night turned black. Alexander was frantic with worry.

'You don't think, she'd try to harm herself, Calum?' he asked, thinking of the cliffs at Tora Point.

Calum shook his head, before he said to Flora, 'Go check if any of her clothes are missin'.'

'Good idea!' said Alexander, as Flora sped off.

When the servant returned, she reported that a few of her dresses seemed to be missing and a small suitcase.

'But where can she have gone at this time of night?' asked Alexander, pacing the drawing-room like a caged lion.

'Here – drink this!' said Calum, handing him a large whisky. 'One thing's sure, we can't do any more searchin' until mornin'.'

'But we can't just sit here!' he exclaimed, waving away the drink.

'There's nothin' else to be done the night!' retorted Calum firmly, pressing the whisky into one of his hands. 'She's not out to harm herself, or she wouldn't have taken anythin' with her. Like it or not, she's made up her mind to take off – somewhere – and all we can do till mornin' is worry and guess.'

CHAPTER SIXTEEN

WHILE Alexander and Calum began a sleepless night, Mhairi Anne said anxiously to Victoria, 'I hope John believed you.' She was seated by the fireside in Victoria's small sitting-room, the darkness outside now complete.

'I'm sure he did,' Victoria assured her from her adjacent seat.

'I hate to think of the worry I am causing,' muttered Mhairi-Anne vexedly.

'As you have said, there was no other way. I am happy to help you.'

Mhairi-Anne smiled at her weakly. 'I will never be able to thank you enough. Staying in Perth for a while, at any rate, will give me time to make plans. I think you are the only true friend I have ever had.'

Victoria shook her head dismissively. 'And I will join you next week. You will not be alone for long.'

Mhairi-Anne nodded. 'Yes – they would be suspicious immediately, if we left together.'

Victoria rose from the chair. 'You rest. I'll make us some tea.'

As Victoria put the kettle on to boil on the stove in her kitchen and laid out crockery on a tray, she wondered at how calm she now felt, after the shock of Mhairi-Anne's revelations this evening. She had come to her, supposedly to say goodbye, but had added that she felt that she owed her the truth before she left the island, as they had been friends. *Never* in her wildest imaginings, could Victoria have anticipated the confessions that followed. Of course, she had often wondered at Mhairi-Anne's unpopularity, but she had imagined that this was the result of petty jealousy among the islanders. Friends, she had said! With James McNair's mistress! Had she ever known this slut? And she had even had the effrontery to imply that she had added Alexander to her list of conquests! Of course, she did not believe her avowals that she was now set to leave the island, to save him from her infamy. The lying hussy obviously had some further devious plan afoot to ensnare him on the mainland. And to think, she herself had been ready to give up Alexander, knowing how he felt about her. She had wanted his happiness more than her own. But how could such a woman ever make him happy? Somehow, she would protect him, Victoria had already determined, feeling in this affirmation a strange, new sense of purpose in her life. She had not rejected his proposal of marriage only to see him degraded by the likes of her!

Consequently, after the initial shock had waned, she had thought quickly, and actively persuaded the woman to go to her hunting lodge, as they had previously planned. Of course, that was probably why she had called this evening, to establish this very arrangement, and she had only felt the need to confess her duplicity, to explain her extraordinary flight from the island perhaps, for fear that the whole dirty story might reach her ears from another source, after her departure. Amazingly, however, Mhairi-Anne had actually seemed to expect that *she* would understand. *Understand!* She must have taken her for a fool – or a guttersnipe, like herself. The very thought of her lying with James McNair and then Alexander made her flesh crawl. But in Perth, she would be able to keep an eye on her and ensure somehow that she did not succeed in renewing her affair with Alexander on the mainland. Of course, she would never tell Alexander, she had assured the pleading Mhairi-Anne. But not for your sake, madam, she had thought viciously!

She smiled, as she returned to the sitting-room and sat the tray down on her tea table. 'You will feel better after this. Then try to sleep. I will wake you when it is time.'

CHAPTER SEVENTEEN

ALEXANDER did not consider going to bed and neither did Calum. The interminable hours of darkness passed with vexing slowness, on a diet of talk, pacing and drinking. Alexander alternated between fits of fear at what might have happened to her, and anger at her inflicting this additional ordeal upon them.

He waited only for the first spiralling streaks of the rising sun to spray the sky, before he saddled the mare and went to search the schoolhouse. The idea that she might have chosen to spend the night there, at the scene of the accident, in some bizarre notion of penance, had occurred to him and Calum agreed that it was probably the most likely place to search first. Calum was to wait at the castle, until he reported back. Then, if necessary, they would proceed elsewhere.

He rode like the devil over the moorland, so that the sun had still not fully risen when he reached the schoolhouse. Having leapt off the horse and left her nibbling on the dewy turf, he walked more cautiously towards the building, not wishing to startle her, if she were inside. In the semi-darkness the place had an eerie quality about it, an atmosphere gorily enhanced by the bloodstain which still marked the ground, where Seorus had fallen.

The door opened at his touch and, as he peered into the dim interior, he cursed himself for not having had the forethought to bring a lamp. Gradually, however, his eyes grew accustomed to the dim light and he searched the building thoroughly. There was no sign of her.

Outside again, he remembered the shed where the desks were stored. Hope rose again in his chest, as he bolted round to it. As soon as he had opened the creaking door, however, he saw immediately she was not there. The interior was crammed with desks and other equipment.

The whole orb of the morning sun was visible on the horizon, as he rode more slowly back to the castle, disappointment giving way to some of his more bizarre notions of the night. Could someone have kidnapped her? There was no sign of a struggle, but she was unpopular. Supposing. . . .

His imaginings were terminated as he saw a dark figure striding purposefully towards the castle, unusual at this time of the morning. He reined to a halt, to peer as the man came closer and realized it was Neil Graham. His heels immediately dug into the mare and he cantered towards him, just as he reached the entrance and Calum came out to greet them.

'I've news for you,' said Graham, glancing from one to the other.

'About Mhairi-Anne?' asked Alexander, swiftly dismounting.

'Aye – I'm playin' "postie".' He produced two letters from his pocket and handed both to Alexander. One was for him, the other for his uncle – both in her handwriting.

'How did you get these?' Alexander demanded.

'You'd better come inside, Neil,' intervened Calum. Alexander tied the mare to a hook on the castle wall and followed the two men into James's study, where the islanders were always received.

'I think you'd better read her letter first,' said Neil. 'Then I'll tell you my part in it.'

Alexander laid the letter for his uncle on his desk and walked to the window with the one addressed to him. His back to them, he ripped open the envelope. He knew it would not be good news and he braced himself as he spread the sheets out before him.

My Dearest Alexander

Had I left this letter in my room, I know you would have tried to stop me before I left the island, and I fear I would not have been strong enough to resist you. Forgive me for all the worry I must already have caused you, but there was no other way.

I think we both knew that we had no realistic chance of finding happiness together and after yesterday's terrible accident, I realized anew that I could do nothing but blight your life. Sometimes, I think the islanders are right about me. I never mean to harm anyone, but inevitably I seem to spread unhappiness and tragedy. I concluded that by leaving immediately, I could perhaps, save us both some pain in the long term. My departure must have shocked you, but I am sure that prolonging our fantasy would only have guaranteed more acute suffering for both of us.

I have written a letter to James, concluding our relationship for reasons you know. The renewed hate of me, which will surely follow Seorus's death, I have offered as additional reason for my swift departure. Your name has not been mentioned, and I beg you not to increase your suffering or his, by revealing our ill-fated love for each other. Nothing can be gained by this now.

I do not think he will tell you about me, even now. He is a proud man and my going will hurt him. Forgive him for deceiving you, Alexander, as you would surely require his forgiveness, if he knew the truth about us. Don't make my going pointless.

I am writing this as I journey on the ferry to the mainland with Neil Graham at the helm. With the prospect of being rid of me, I knew this was one favour I could ask of him.

Don't seek me on the mainland, as I plan to change my name and travel. When I knew you were downstairs, I took the purse from your room, which you gave me the other night. I need the funds to ensure distance between us and the immediate necessities in life. One day, I hope to return this loan to you. I took it only to free you!

By the time you read this, I should be far away. I hope Neil

Graham keeps his promise to deliver this to you. He realizes there is something between us, I think, and despises me all the more for it, but, in these circumstances, I think he will comply, if only for your sake.

Forgive me, my dearest love,

Mhairi-Anne

Alexander stuffed the letter in his pocket and stared dazedly out of the window for some time, before fury came to his rescue. Graham had conspired in her departure! He turned towards him and Calum again, fighting an urge to drag the man from the chair and thrash him.

Had Graham's expression suggested anything like complacency, he might well have forgotten the seniority of his years. But the sobriety of his face gave no hint that he was rejoicing in this moment. On the contrary, as he looked up at Alexander, he said immediately, 'I'm sorry – I couldn't get here sooner.'

Alexander sat down next to Calum and across from Graham. 'You had no business taking her to the mainland!' he said tightly. 'You knew what she was about.'

'All I know is she came to me last night and said she wanted to leave Tora and I welcomed it.'

'She was with you all last night?'

'Aye!' he lied, just as Miss Victoria had told him, when he had picked her up there.

Alexander's eyes blazed at him. 'Wait till my uncle hears of this.'

'I only did as she wanted.'

'As *you* wanted!'

'I'll not deny that to you, nor your uncle. I heard about Seorus when I got back from Mount Tora. I thought at first she'd realized finally she'd better leave.'

'At first?'

'I guessed later – there was more to it.' He looked at Alexander, daring him to admit what had been going on. When

Alexander continued to sit tight-tipped, glaring back at him, he added, 'Of course, I won't be sayin' anythin' about my thoughts – to anybody.'

'The less gossip, the better for all concerned,' intervened Calum soothingly. 'I think, if you've said all you came for, Neil. . . .'

Graham stood up. 'Aye – I'd better be off.'

Alexander stayed seated morosely in his chair and Graham touched him lightly on the shoulder as he passed. 'I'm sorry, believe me, but it's for the best.'

Calum returned from seeing Neil off, to find Alexander had not moved. 'What does she say?' Alexander dug out the crumpled letter. 'Here – read it. There's nothing you can't know.'

Calum extracted a monocle from his pocket and, fixing it in one eye, read the epistle, while Alexander now sat forward covering his face with his hands, as he tried to come to terms with the fact that he had lost her.

'She took money?' queried Calum, as he read.

Alexander nodded grimly.

'I wondered how she'd manage. Was it much? I don't understand this bit.'

'It's of no importance how it came about. But, yes, it was quite a sum. Enough to ensure I'll never find her.'

Calum read on to the end of the letter. 'Well, that's that!' he muttered sadly, taking the monocle from his eye. He paused thoughtfully, before adding, 'Will you take the golden opportunity she's handed you?'

'Of conveniently forgetting I ever loved her?' responded Alexander wearily.

'Of avoidin' at least some of the strife!'

'So I forget my uncle deceived me, while I deceive him?'

'That's the way she wants it. That's why she did it – to avoid messin' up your life.'

'The only problem is she's all I want in life and now she's gone. And don't tell me I'll get over it in time, for God's sake!'

He ran his hand distractedly through his hair. 'I'm going to bed. I'm exhausted.'

He stood up, as Calum silently handed back the letter.

'I'm sorry for snapping!' he muttered. 'I promise – I'll think over what you've said.'

'I know you will, laddie!' Calum stood up, too, and clapped him on the back. 'Come on! We'll both feel the better for a bit of sleep. I've warned Neil Graham to say nothin' to James on the ferry tomorrow. I'll meet him at the harbour myself. By then, you'll know what you want to do.'

In his room, Alexander looked briefly at his bedside table, where he had last deposited his 'emergency fund'. If only he had noticed it was gone, he might have stopped her, he thought despairingly, or anticipated her flight. If only. . . . His mind throbbed to these words, until finally a blessed sleep brought temporary oblivion.

CHAPTER EIGHTEEN

HAD Alexander still harboured any doubts about following Mhairi-Anne's wishes, they would certainly have vanished when he saw his uncle in the drawing-room of the castle on Thursday afternoon, after Calum had fetched him from the harbour. He looked to have aged ten years since he had last seen him; his normally erect posture was stooped, and his formerly lively eyes held a brooding sadness and were red-rimmed.

'The wind,' he explained, self-consciously, but Alexander knew better. Calum had been gone a long time and he had taken the other letter written by Mhairi-Anne.

As they shook hands, he thought momentarily that here was his rival. But if this had been the case, there was no competition. His uncle was already vanquished by events which had overtaken him in his absence, and, in any case, the prize had been lost to both of them. Still, he was surprised by the level of pity which arose in his heart, as James endeavoured to account for his devastation through references to Seorus's death and manufactured indignation at the loss of the children's teacher.

'Of course, it was this horrible accident which drove her to it,' he murmured, evading Alexander's eyes. 'She just couldn't face another round of gossip and hatred.'

He did not linger long in the drawing-room after his arrival. Professing weariness after a rough crossing, he disappeared to his room to rest before the start of Seorus's wake, and left Alexander and Calum alone.

'He's read her letter, I take it?' queried Alexander, as they sat having tea on a sofa adjacent to the fireplace.

'Aye – he didn't let me see it, but it seems to have been just as she said: she's kept you out of it.'

'I still can't believe I may never see her again,' murmured Alexander, his cloak of normality dropping to reveal the wretchedness which had enveloped him since her disappearance.

Calum gave him an encouraging nudge. 'You've done the right thing. No point in kickin' a dog when he's down and bashin' yourself in the process.'

Alexander nodded. 'I actually feel sorry for him. I suppose it's better than feeling sorry for myself.'

'You won't have to keep up a front much longer,' revealed Calum. 'He'll tell you about it himself, when he gets his breath back, but it looks like you'll be goin' home soon. Your brother's ill.'

'Did he visit Strathcairn?'

'Aye, called in overnight. Your father wants you back.'

'Eric wasn't well when I left, but it's not anything serious, surely?'

'Not urgent, James said, but serious enough apparently. That's all he told me before he read Mhairi-Anne's letter.'

'My father tends to panic where Eric's concerned,' Alexander responded thoughtfully. 'It's probably something and nothing.'

While it had occurred to him over the past twenty-four hours that he might do well to quit the island as soon as possible now, that feeling had been confused by a reluctance to lose contact with all the memories he had stored here. Earlier, he had visited her room, touched her clothes, lain on her bed in an ecstasy of bitter-sweet recollection and wallowed in her ghostly presence everywhere. On the mainland, there would be nothing to remind him and he was not certain how he could bear that yet, but it looked as if he no longer had a choice.

That evening, for two hours, the walls of the castle reverberated to the haunting sound of Gaelic voices, raised to psalm singing over the body of Seores Dhu, lying now on a high trestle in the castle library, a suitably sombre room, seldom used, where everyone congregated.

There was a constant stream of islanders, coming with their little packages, to pay their respects. Some older islanders, who had known Seorus all of his life, had journeyed back from the Mount Tora pastures to be there and Alexander was amazed at the evident popularity of the man, who, for a substantial portion of his life, had wandered the island intoxicated. But, in a way, he had been like everyone's child, at some time or another. His parents, also retarded, had died in his youth. He had done jobs for people all over Tora and stories about him abounded, while everyone forgot his nuisance value, prior to his installation at the castle.

The ordeal of the event for Alexander was intensified by the minister's constant harping back to Seorus's recent conversion from alcohol. Morrison waxed lyrical on this point in between psalms, while Alexander waited tensely on a mention of Mhairi-Anne's name, fearing he might leap and kill him. But, perhaps, James or Calum had warned him not to dwell on the circumstances surrounding the accident. In his diatribe, Seorus might well have been a warrior, killed heroically in battle, and Alexander heaved a huge sigh of relief. From the look of exhaustion on his uncle's face, he felt similarly affected, and the fact that James had curtailed the wake to one evening only was another blessing.

Later, he found that he was to be spared also the ordeal of the funeral the next day, as his uncle had actually arranged a special ferry for his departure. Eric had tuberculosis. His father was distraught and wanted him home immediately: the prognosis was not good.

'I'm sorry, I should have told you right away on my return,' said James apologetically over dinner, 'but with all this business with Mhairi-Anne and Seorus – it's been some homecoming.'

Alexander nodded distractedly, still reeling at the possibility that his brother might die. They had never been close – never been able to understand one another – but the idea of losing him was unbelievable and vexing. But surely, he would recover.

'Don't punish yourself because you've never got on with him, m'boy,' advised James soberly. 'God knows, David and I never hit it off, but I wouldn't like to lose him – that goes without saying.'

'There must be something they can do,' muttered Alexander.

'I understand Calum spoke to you about your inheritance,' said James, changing the subject.

Alexander nodded.

'I know it's premature, but you'll have a lot more power in your hands, if you also come into Strathcairn.'

Still feeling waves of guilt wash over him, as he recalled his frequent quarrels with his brother, Alexander responded, 'I really don't want to discuss this now, Uncle. Especially, not after a wake.'

'No, of course not. I trust you anyway, m'boy! You've grown a bond with this island, as I did.'

Alexander looked at him in an agony of silence. Trust – if only he knew. The sooner he got off this island, the better, he realized anew.

There was someone else he had to see before he departed, however – Victoria. The following morning, after an emotional farewell with his uncle and promises to write regularly, he asked Calum to let him down at the library, *en route* to the harbour.

She was in the process of stacking a new package of books on a shelf, when he entered and, as she came round to the front counter, only then did it strike him as strange that she had not sought further information about Mhairi-Anne, after John's dramatic visit on the night of her disappearance.

'Flora has been keeping me informed,' she explained, when he questioned whether she had heard of her departure. 'You must have been frantic with worry. It is . . . unfortunate that she chose to leave in such a fashion, but I cannot criticize, as I did much the same thing in coming here.'

'We were glad to hear she had not perished somewhere.'

'I suppose she was very upset after Seorus's death.' She paused awkwardly. 'I confess I do not understand it all. I was rather annoyed that she did not even say goodbye.'

'You must feel she's let you down, after the plans you discussed and the efforts you made regarding sale of her work.'

She smiled tightly. 'It's of no account, really. She must have had her reasons.'

'I expect you will be leaving soon yourself.'

'Next week, all being well.'

'Is it possible she may contact you on the mainland?' he queried, hopefully.

'What makes you think that?'

'The paintings you sent to your solicitor.'

'I doubt it. I'm afraid I had more hope they could be sold than ever she did. Of course, I will contact him again and have them returned to your uncle, as there is no point now in proceeding with any sale.'

'Could I ask you to get in touch with me at Strathcairn, if you ever hear from her?'

'You're going home?'

'Today – now – in fact. My brother is ill.'

'Oh!'

For a moment, Alexander thought she might burst into tears, but she controlled herself. To his relief, the agitation passed and she said with admirable calm, 'I hope you have a safe voyage and, of course, if I ever hear from Mhairi-Anne, I will get in touch.' She paused before adding, 'I cannot imagine such a circumstance is likely, however. We never actually discussed the precise location of my residence in Perth, so that she will not know where to locate me.'

He nodded. 'I must go now.'

She came from behind the library counter and walked with

him to the door, where she gripped one of his arms tightly. 'Take care of yourself.'

He tilted her head to kiss her lightly on the lips. This was almost her undoing.

'Will . . . I ever . . . see you again?' she murmured, her voice breaking noticeably.

'Write to me,' he said, 'when you are settled. You know the estate, I believe. If I can ever give you any assistance, you only need to ask.'

'Who does not know of Strathcairn?' She smiled brightly and, as he patted her hand, she released his arm.

Climbing back on to the dogcart outside, he looked back to wave, but already the library door was closed behind her.

As they journeyed on to the harbour, Alexander looked back at the castle and the surrounding moorland, which had grown rich with approaching summer, and was now splashed with colourful clusters of wild flowers. His uncle had been right about one thing. He had developed a bond with this island and its hardy, unforgiving people. Quite why this was, he did not fully comprehend. It was a world apart from the mainland and the luxury of Strathcairn – a world in which class differences were relatively insignificant, and life was a daily struggle against encroaching death. In a few unforgettable weeks, he had known the happiest and the most miserable days of his life here, and he had been changed irrevocably by the experience. At this stage, he could not imagine ever being happy again.

PART II

STRATHCAIRN

CHAPTER NINETEEN

July 1897

'YOUR father seems more like his old self these days,' said Rowena, Lady McNair, as she walked on the arm of her son around the lush gardens of Strathcairn. It was just after dinner and the air was heavy with the scent of her favourite roses. She loved the peacefulness of the gardens at this time of night and she hoped that Alexander would confide in her. 'He could not have coped since Eric's death without you,' she added, when he did not respond.

Absently, he patted her hand. 'I've still a lot to learn.'

'You've done wonders! It can't have been easy for you.'

'On the contrary, I enjoy being busy.'

The estate entailed thousands of verdant acres, the administrative demands of which, alone, as Alexander was now learning, were immense. Income derived from numerous tenant farmers, fishing, game hunting and shooting, and timber had made Sir David McNair into one of the richest lairds in the country, and this, allied to sound business investments at home and abroad, accounted for the fact that the McNair family was listed as one of the wealthiest in Great Britain.

As heir to such a fortune, Alexander was now among the most

eligible of bachelors – a state which his parents were increasingly eager to see him change, to ensure the succession. His lack of interest in socializing, however, was now concerning his mother in particular, as she recalled his former exuberance and she had become increasingly convinced of late, that he was deeply unhappy for some reason.

'Now that Isobel is out of mourning,' Lady McNair resumed, referring to Eric's wife, who still lived at Strathcairn, 'we will be able to have guests much more frequently and parties, like we used to do.'

Alexander glanced down at his mother, as her voice tailed off. 'None of us is ready yet for entertaining on a grand scale.'

'I worry about you – all the more so, since losing Eric. You're young – you need to get back to enjoying life. I know you took his death as hard as any of us, but we all need to join the living again.'

After his return from Tora, he and his brother had become extraordinarily close over the few remaining months of his life, perhaps because both of their attitudes had altered, for very different reasons. 'You mustn't fret about me,' he said now to his mother. I'm as healthy as an ox.'

'But you're not happy, are you?'

'What makes you say that?' countered Alexander.

'Oh – lots of things – little things.' She smiled up at him persuasively. 'Tell me what's troubling you.'

They had arrived at a little arbor in the garden with a bench under an old willow tree, his mother's favourite spot, and they sat down. Before he had gone to Tora, they had always been extremely close. Since then, with the trauma surrounding Eric's death and the need for him to step into his brother's place, there had been little time for the intimate talks they had formerly enjoyed, or so he had told himself. Perhaps, he had avoided them, knowing eventually she would ask this very question.

'I've been thinking about you a lot, lately,' she revealed, when still she had no answer. 'I noticed a change in you when you returned from Tora, but, at the time, I put it down to Eric's illness. Now I'm not so sure.'

He smiled at her evasively. 'Father is delighted with the change in me.'

'Not entirely!'

'What has he been saying?'

'Oh, he's very pleased with your new attitude to work, but he agrees there's something amiss. I call it "sparkle".'

He laughed and kissed her cheek. 'You sparkle enough for all of us.'

'It's no joking matter,' she admonished lightly. 'Did something happen on Tora? You've never really told us anything of your visit.'

'Of course, I have,' he countered, his face sobering.

'Something happened there to change you so, Alexander,' she insisted, 'and it's time you spoke to someone.'

He rose abruptly from the seat and began plucking leaves from the overhanging willow. Every emotion connected with Tora had been locked up inside him for so long, it seemed pointless to dredge up the old pain. Or was he afraid? He felt his mother's hand on his arm and he looked round at her anxious face.

'Please, Alexander! Tell me what's wrong.' Tears, never far away since Eric's death, stood again in her eyes and he put his arms around her, hating as always to see her distressed. The stunning beauty of her youth had mellowed through the years into fragile elegance that still turned men's heads and Alexander adored her.

In this tight embrace, he whispered, as if testing his own emotional strength, 'I think I fell in love on Tora. It's over, but I can't forget her.'

She did not move to see the anguish on his face. It was enough to hear the pain in his voice and for several minutes, she allowed him simply to hold her.

Eventually, emotions in control, he led her back to the bench, where they both sat down once more.

'So, now you know,' he continued with calm deliberation. 'I think my problem is called "unrequited love" in ladies' circles.'

'Was this woman a guest of your uncle?'

'Something like that. It's of no importance who she was.'

'You say you lost her – how? Was she not in love with you?'

'On the contrary, she loved me too much,' said Alexander cynically, these words imprinted on his brain.

'You are making it all sound very mysterious, Alexander. I don't understand.'

He shrugged. 'There is no mystery. She left the island suddenly. I have no idea where she is now.'

'Did you quarrel?'

'It's a rather complicated story, Mama. The point is she's gone.'

'She's not married, is she?' she queried worriedly.

'No – come – let's forget about it.'

'But the point is, you've not forgotten about it in all these months, Alexander! You must find her, sort out the problem – whatever it is – if she means so very much to you.'

He smiled grimly, knowing that if his mother knew the whole truth, she would certainly not be advocating such action.

'It is the only thing to do,' insisted Lady McNair. 'There must be some means of tracking her down.'

'Even if I did track her down, as you say, there are other difficulties.'

'I cannot imagine what you mean, my dear,' she continued, 'but it seems to me that most difficulties in relationships can be sorted out, providing, of course, she is free, as you say and – well – I am sure you would not have found her so appealing in the first instance, if she were not . . . er . . . suitable.'

A low laugh rumbled in his throat at his mother's delicate snobbery. If only she knew. . . .

'First, you must locate her,' continued Lady McNair, warming to her theme. 'Has James no idea where she is?'

He shook his head. Although he and his uncle had corresponded regularly since his visit, her name had never been raised.

'What about friends you might approach?

His thoughts turned to Victoria. According to his uncle, she had left the island not long after his departure, but she had never written to him. Was she still in Perth, he wondered? He should have taken her address perhaps, but at the time he had not really wanted to pursue the association and the only reason he would wish to see her now was her possible link to Mhairi-Anne. But surely, she would have contacted him, if there had been any news, and looking her up at this juncture could raise old memories he would rather forget.

'Is there anyone, you might contact?' pursued his mother.

'No – I don't think so.'

She sighed deeply and he patted her hand.

'I told you so you would stop worrying about me, Mama. Now you know – let's leave it there.'

Later in his room, however, Alexander's thoughts returned to Victoria. Was it worth trying to locate her on the off-chance she might have heard something? Perhaps his uncle knew her address. On impulse, he sat down at his desk and wrote a letter to James, consisting of the usual news concerning his increasing involvement in the management of Strathcairn. And in the last paragraph, he casually posed the question regarding Victoria's current whereabouts.

It could do no harm asking, he thought, as he sealed the envelope for posting, even though he would probably not follow any information through. The last thing he wanted to do was become involved with Victoria again and his mother's comments had highlighted all too clearly that even if he ever did manage to locate Mhairi-Anne, any continuance of the relationship between them would pose a whole set of new problems.

CHAPTER TWENTY

LIKE Tora, Strathcairn was also a world unto itself – in a sense, as much apart from the rest of the country as the island was – but while the appeal of Tora lay in the rugged, indomitable grandeur of naked land pitched against the elements, here nature had co-operated with all her lush finery, to produce excellence in scenery and a paradise for man to inhabit.

Guests on the estate never failed to be impressed. From its huge crested gates, past the granite lodge that guarded the family privacy on to the long winding drive that led up to the mansion house itself, all bespoke a heritage that included aristocracy. For anyone bowling along the driveway in a coach, marvellous views punctuated densely wooded sections, to surprise and enchant. Forested hillsides, open fields and vast meadows filled with wild flowers were all in evidence and, as the estate included the turbulent River Cairn, gullies and waterfalls added to nature's variety. In winter, the river was a torrent of brown water, heavily stained by the peat in the soil and brushed by white foam, as it bounced aggressively against the boulders in its path. Now in summer, salmon leapt in abundance against its strong current and trout multiplied in its sleepy pools. Fox, rabbit, deer, red grouse and pheasant, along with a myriad of trees and crops thrived on its rich red soil. Most people found it hard to credit that this jewel of nature existed a mere ten miles or so from the harshly industrial city of Dundee.

Alexander had never counted the exact number of rooms in

the house itself, but it was a palatial residence by any standards. A granite structure with a series of turrets, enormous arched windows, crow-stepped gables, and broad, pillared entrance, it was entirely congruous with its surroundings. A backdrop of gently undulating wooded hills added perspective to its glorious setting, while its splendid gardens, with flowers, vegetables and fruit in abundance, were surrounded by high walls, shaded by overhanging trees, to add to the family's seclusion.

Many of the rooms in the mansion were large and airy, the main ones in use by the family all leading off the great hall, where elegant balls had been held for the district over many years. A massive staircase wound upstairs to bedrooms with huge brass bedsteads or dark four-posters. Dressing-rooms and beautiful gothic-styled bathrooms with the latest in plumbing equipment were attached to the main suites, one of which Alexander occupied. All were reached by a long broad corridor that ran from one end of the house to the other, so that visitors rarely got lost. At the back, on two levels, ground floor and basement, were the kitchen, scullery, cellar, store rooms and a myriad of servants' quarters.

Lady McNair, whose family pedigree was even more impressive than her husband's, ensured the house and gardens were kept in immaculate order. Although demanding of efficiency, she was held in the highest esteem by everyone. Despite the fact that she was inevitably class conscious and had been cosseted all of her life, she had an intuitive understanding of people from most walks of life and a shrewd brain. Behind the scenes, Sir David, commander-in-chief, to whom everyone ultimately looked for orders, was freqently manipulated by his wife, without his ever knowing it.

While an army of workers serviced the estate, a veritable regiment of servants catered for the family inside the house. They were well accustomed to servants flitting around them in the dining-room, like silent bees, and their discussions were rarely inhibited by fears for their privacy: everyone who worked indoors was always carefully vetted by Lady McNair, who used a reputable agency in Dundee for this purpose.

'The Perth Highland Games are next week,' said Sir David over breakfast, one morning almost a fortnight after Alexander's discussion with his mother in the garden. 'We missed it last year, of course, but we should put in an appearance this time, I think.'

'How do you feel about it?' asked Lady McNair of her daughter-in-law, who sat next to Alexander.

Isobel was generally a quiet creature – insipid, many might have claimed – but she could appear attractive when she added a little colour to her sallow complexion and wore her light-brown hair in a more flattering style than its customary severe chignon. She and Eric had been ideally suited; she had never questioned his judgement and, consequently, they had never rowed. Prior to her husband's death, her relationship with Alexander had been distant, to say the least. She had found his manly good looks intimidating and his sometimes risqué sense of humour bordering on the offensive. Well aware of this, he had often taken quiet delight in teasing her, but no more. Now he felt sorry for his sister-in-law, left as she was in a kind of limbo at Strathcairn, with no child to justify her status, and little chance of finding another husband, before her fertility and her looks completely faded. Consequently, they had grown closer over the past year and, on the few occasions she had been in public, he had been her escort.

Faced now with Lady McNair's question, she turned hesitantly towards him. 'Will you go, Alexander?'

'Why not!' he responded with manufactured enthusiasm and taking an unspoken cue from his mother, whom he had been trying especially hard to impress with his zest for life, since their conversation in the garden.

Lady McNair was not fooled, but her husband was. 'Good, we'll make it a real family occasion. Of course, we'll be expected to present some of the prizes, Alexander.' He paused before adding more soberly, 'Eric always shared the task with me.'

A gloom settled suddenly like an insect on the table and Alexander forced a note of joviality into his voice. 'You can have the caber throwers then, Papa – I'll have the highland dancers!'

His father snorted. 'Trust you to want the ones with the pretty legs.'

'David – really!' exclaimed his wife with feigned severity, while Isobel's pale cheeks momentarily coloured a healthy pink.

As Alexander and his father left the breakfast-table that morning, to deal first with the inevitable paperwork of the day, a shiver of apprehension traversed his spine, as he conduded 'fate' or 'choice' was again beckoning him. The day before, a letter had arrived from his uncle, giving him Victoria's address in Perth. Since then, he had been debating the wisdom of either writing to her or seeing her once again, given the unlikely chance that she had any news.

Now, however, it seemed almost as if destiny was signalling to him to take this opportunity next week, when he would already be in Perth for the games.

CHAPTER TWENTY-ONE

THE men in the necessary full kilt regalia and the ladies dressed in all their summer finery, the McNairs made a handsome group as they set off in their gleaming, comfortably sprung coach the following week, to attend the games in Perth.

Alexander had quite taken the breath away from the young female servants, who watched his departure with particular interest, and, for a brief moment, Isobel forgot she was a lady and gaped! The muscles of his legs were finely tuned by his daily rides on his favourite black stallion and his breadth of shoulder, allied to his height, made the outfit into a striking fashion statement, instead of the comedy item, it sometimes appeared on shorter men.

In the trunk of the coach, he had stored an overnight valise, containing a change of clothes, should he decide to extend his visit to Perth, for the purpose of visiting Victoria. While he wanted to see her for his own selfish reasons, he feared the effect of such a visit on her, and, bearing in mind that he had already grievously wronged her, he had asked himself the question – how would he feel if Mhairi-Anne turned up on his doorstep, only to turn away again? It did not bear thinking about! On the other hand, the fact that Victoria had not written to him suggested, perhaps, that he was long forgotten. At her age, he had often thought himself in love and it was possible now that she would simply see him as an old friend. Even allowing for this positive outcome, however, and for the unlikely eventuality that she had news of Mhairi-Anne's whereabouts, was he not simply asking for further turmoil in his life and that of his family, if he then chose to pursue any lead? And yet . . . the remote possibility of simply seeing her again tantalized and tormented him. In essence, therefore, he could not make up his mind what to do and he felt as if he were awaiting another bolt from the blue to spur him on.

The McNairs were immediately conducted to the central platform with other dignitaries, when they arrived in good time for the start of the games. Lady McNair was delighted to be asked to cut the red ribbon, which marked the beginning of a huge range of competitive activities, including all sorts of athletics, tug-of-war, caber tossing, barrel throwing, Highland dancing and the ancient game of shinty.

In addition, the games provided a competitive arena for prize animals, with enormous bulls lumbering forth to great applause and thoroughbred horses drawing gasps of admiration from onlookers. Fairground amenities were also available on the fringes of the great park and, after the opening rituals were over, the McNairs were free to wander until the prize-giving ceremony at the end of the games, when they were again obliged to appear on the platform.

Lady McNair was proud to walk on the arm of her handsome son, who drew eyes wherever they went, while Isobel had the dubious pleasure of Sir David's company.

'What was the purpose of the valise you stored in the coach, by the way?' she asked Alexander, as they strolled along.

'I may stay overnight here and return tomorrow,' he revealed reluctantly.

'For what purpose? You will have a much more comfortable ride home with us than on a hired coach.'

'I thought I might visit a friend?'

'Oh? A mysterious friend, by any chance?'

'You don't know her.'

'You're being very evasive, Alexander!'

'I'm approaching thirty, Mother, and you're being rather nosy!'

'Is this young woman anything to do with our discussion the other evening?' she pursued, not daunted, and glancing up at him shrewdly.

'I don't even know if I will go.'

'Then she does concern that business on Tora?'

'You're impossible!'

She stopped him with a gentle tug on his arm. 'You are not fooling me one bit, Alexander,' she admonished quietly. 'If you do not wish to discuss her at this juncture – fine. But don't hesitate to investigate. For your own good, you must resolve this matter.'

'Fine – I'll go! Happy now?'

She smiled and they walked on. 'Your father and I would like nothing better than to see you married and settled for the future with someone you care about. You understand how important this is for all of us, now Eric is gone?'

'Of course, Mother, but these things cannot happen to order.'

'They will never happen, if you go on pining for this mysterious individual you met on Tora.'

After a buffet luncheon in a marquee, set up to cater for all the special guests invited to the games, the afternoon wore on to the final competitions and prize-giving. Standing beside his father on the platform for the first time, to hand over cups and awards to all the winners, as Eric had done, was emotionally trying for both of them and they were glad when they heard the last wail of the pipes, which signalled the end of the games.

On their return to the coach, Alexander discovered that his mother had already advised the others that he would be staying in the city. Consequently, he was allowed no more time for hesitation and they dropped him off at the The Grand Hotel, before continuing on their journey back to Strathcairn.

Although he had thought he might make the visit that evening, he shortly learned at the hotel that the residence was in a glen, some two miles beyond the city. Of course, Victoria had described it as a hunting lodge, he recalled, and this would necessarily require a country location. He decided, therefore, to arrange coach hire for the following morning, have dinner and an early night, as opposed to appearing on her doorstep, like a ghost in the twilight.

The next morning, he set off at ten o'clock sharp, as planned, with the coach and coachman at his disposal for the entire day. The journey proved relatively smooth over the initial stretches of road, but, as they moved into the countryside, he realized he was spoiled by the coaches at Strathcairn. Over the last mile, he was bumped and jolted back and forth, so that he was relieved when the coachman finally signalled their arrival.

What would she say? How would she react? His heart beat feverishly to these questions, as he climbed down from the coach in front of a small but solid grey-stone residence, fronted by a tiny garden that was separated by a narrow pathway to the front door. In fact, it appeared more like a cottage than a hunting lodge, he thought, but he supposed the description rather depended upon the use to which such a building was put. Certainly, the surrounding countryside was attractive, with low sweeping hills and woodland, but he wondered how she coped with such isolation.

Evidently, the coach had attracted her attention. As he walked up the pathway, he glimpsed a face momentarily at the window, so that he did not bother to knock. She appeared, however, a long time coming and he was about to raise his hand to the knocker, when finally the door opened.

Her expression betrayed astonishment, delight and some other emotion he could not define. They embraced warmly, before she ushered him into the small front parlour of the house.

'How did you find me?' she asked, her smile trembling. 'But I forget my manners. Let me take your jacket and please sit down.'

She looked much older than he remembered – a mature woman – he thought. Her face had lost its elfin sharpness and she had filled out elsewhere. If anything, however, she was more attractive.

Finally, she sat, too, and he rapidly explained how he had obtained her address. 'As you had not written, I thought I would look you up, when I was in the district.'

'I see. On business?'

'We were at the Highland Games.'

'We?'

'My mother, father and sister-in-law.'

'They are not with you now?' She glanced anxiously towards the window and the waiting coach.

'No – they've gone back to Strathcairn. Of course, you may not know of my brother's death.' For the next ten minutes, he related how his life had changed over the past year and while he was doing most of the talking, she seemed relatively at ease. 'But what about you?' he said eventually, hoping now to steer the conversation around to the purpose of his visit.

'I am well – very well.'

'Did you come straight here from Tora?'

'Yes – I've been here more than a year now.'

'I was surprised to find it so isolated.'

'It is not so very far from Perth.'

'How do you manage for provisions?'

'My father and I had long been on friendly terms with a farmer, John Linton, who lives further up the glen. He is able to supply me with milk, bread, vegetables, poultry and so on and he runs a market stall in Perth along with his two sons, so that his cart is back and forth several times a week in summer. They all call in when they are passing and I can travel to Perth with them, if need be.

'But it must be, er . . . lonely here – especially in winter – I would imagine,' he suggested tentatively.

'Sometimes – yes – but I forget my manners again. Would you like some tea?'

Before he could refuse, she was on her feet once more and another ten fruitless minutes elapsed, until she sat down to pour. He noticed then that her hand trembled quite violently and she appeared breathless with her efforts. This visit had been a serious mistake, he concluded despondently. Whether she was still in love with him or not, he was clearly causing her emotional distress, and the idea of raising Mhairi-Anne's name seemed guaranteed to make things even more awkward.

The child's cry had the incongruity of thunder in the room. His astonishment, allied to her knowing gasp, propelled them both to their feet, like puppets. In the process, tea was spilled; a cup crashed to the floor and, as the crying spiralled, high and insistent, she fled from the room.

He followed more slowly, feeling suddenly as if his legs trod water, while his mind reeled against the intelligence hammering on his brain. Memories flashed like peals of accusing laughter: a freak summer day: a white sandy beach; mindless kisses; and a careless thrill all too eagerly forgotten. The explosion of images left him winded, as he gazed incredulously at the proof of it all. In the small bedroom, she stood holding a baby, about six months old, her eyes almost as large as its tiny face.

She recovered more swiftly than he did. The child, a boy, from the blue knitted jacket he wore, stopped crying as abruptly as he had begun. Gently, she laid him back in the cradle, and, with only a moment's hesitation, she swept past Alexander, who stood dumb, back supported on the door jamb.

There was no counting the minutes he remained there – glancing occasionally at the infant – not daring to approach him, lest his face scream the knowledge he was still struggling to assimilate. When he did move tentatively towards the crib, the child lay peaceably clutching a rattle and gazing benignly up at him. There was not the moment of direful recognition he feared. Apart from several wisps of very black hair, he saw no resemblance to Victoria or himself. When the child smiled up at him indifferently, however, tears started to his eyes and he backed away to the adjacent bed to sit taking deep calming breaths. This was his son! He knew it without any need for corroboration. What a confounded fool he had been – or what a blackguard! All along, he had simply refused to contemplate that a child could possibly come from such regretted madness. His humiliation and remorse were complete.

Eventually, outwardly composed, he returned to the parlour, where he found that she had cleared up the mess of tea and was sitting awating him tremulously. As he sat down, he said slowly, 'I take it this child is mine.'

It was an acknowledgement of fact, not a question, but she responded defensively. 'Do you doubt it?'

'No . . . no . . . but why didn't you contact me?'

She rose suddenly from the chair, to pace to the window and, with her back to him, she answered, 'I didn't believe you would want to know.' Swiftly, she then turned to face him, her hands clasped tightly in front of her. 'You are clearly not happy to find out you are a father.'

'Under these circumstances, who would be? The shame of it is I am so shocked. I have been a thoughtless idiot – never really considering this possibility. But that is beside the point.'

'Is it? I have been happy looking after your child.'

'Alone, unmarried, hiding from the world in this place! How can you say that?'

'I am not hiding from the world, as you put it,' came the proud retort. 'I live here out of necessity.'

'Then all the more reason for you to have contacted me.'

'So that you could hide your son away in some more suitable accommodation?' she queried, tartly.

He stood up and moved towards her to grasp her clasped hands in his. 'So we could be married – as we should have been when it happened.'

'Out of necessity!' she retorted bitterly.

'Victoria – I will not try to lie to you. I do not want to start out that way and you are too sensitive and intelligent to believe sudden avowals of love, in any case. But I care about you and many successful marriages do not begin with love, as we understand it. I accepted your refusal before, but, in these circumstances, you must think again.' For the first time, he saw doubt in her expression and he pressed the advantage. 'I insist upon it! You cannot possibly expect me to leave you here.'

Even as he spoke these words, his mind raced at the ramifications ahead of them. Much as his parents would dearly love a grandson, in these circumstances there would be hell to pay. The scandal of a belated marriage to a woman who had already borne him a son would reverberate throughout the district like an earthquake. He had, however, essentially no other choice than to brazen it out and by the time his son came of age, the gossip would be long forgotten. To ride away now and forget they existed was an impossibility. Equally so, the idea of beginning a lifetime of concealment, secretly paying her to bring up a son he could never acknowledge, was abhorrent to his nature, and, in any case, everything about her proud attitude suggested she would not accept such dubious assistance.

His mother had told him to resolve the past. In his wildest dreams he had not anticipated such a discovery would inform any resolution of his experience on Tora, but, effectively, Mhairi-Anne must now be dead to him. He would have a son he could love and a wife who deserved his every affection. And, he must never raise her name to Victoria, lest she ever suspect the real selfish purpose of his visit.

Seated by the fireside again, he gradually overcame her protests.

'What will your parents think of us?' she queried fearfully. 'They have surely had enough grief over the past year year. I do not think I can face them!'

'Initially, I will see them alone. Of course, they will be shocked . . . angry, perhaps, at first, but with Eric gone, the consequences may not be as dire as they might have been. They long for a grandson and he will be a great influence in their final attitude What is his name, by the way?'

'We called him Alex.'

'We?'

'We . . . I mean my midwife, Hannah and I, decided on the name. My solicitor secured her services. She lived here during the crucial months.'

'The child was born here?'

'Yes – but I was not alone.'

'Good God, Victoria! You should have had the attendance of a doctor.'

'All went according to plan. You have a healthy son.'

He nodded, his face giving way to a smile, as he experienced only now his first surge of joy in fatherhood. A son! He still could not quite believe it. 'It is all settled then!' he concluded, grasping her hands in his.

She smiled jerkily. 'I will marry you – but not for my sake, although . . . although I still hold a great regard for you. We will be together for Alex. I cannot deny him this chance, but if your parents should—'

'I will deal with my parents!' he intervened determinedly. 'Of course, I want their approval, but it is my decision. You will leave here with me today.'

'But that is impossible!'

'Why?'

'I . . . I thought you would wish to see your parents first.'

'I will, but that does not mean I have to leave you here. There is a secluded house empty on the estate at the moment. You can stay there with Alex until things are settled.'

'But . . . but. . . .' She evidently struggled to find further objections. 'I will have to leave a letter for John Linton, and pack.'

He laughed. 'Get busy then, while I get to know my son. I will tell the coachman we leave for Strathcairn in two hours.'

As Alexander held his son for the first time in his arms, some of the bleakness that had permeated his heart, since his return from Tora, lifted. This had to be enough, he thought.

CHAPTER TWENTY-TWO

THEY departed from the glen early in the afternoon, the letter for John Linton left sticking in the letterbox and the coachman bemused to find that his passengers had multiplied by three.

'Have you locked everything up?' queried Alexander, as he helped her inside.

'No – there is only one key and John Linton may need access. I've left the key for him to lock up, once he receives my message.'

The rocking motion of the coach suited Alex admirably and he slept peacefully for the entire journey, but by the time they reached Strathcairn, Victoria felt quite ill, apparently through nerves or travel sickness. At the gates, Alexander swiftly descended to obtain the keys for Firtree Cottage – the empty house on the estate, which, until recently, had been occupied by their forestry manager, who had retired, but was yet to be replaced. George, the lodge-keeper, eyed the occupants of the coach with more than a little curiosity, but Alexander ignored his unspoken questions, as he took the keys he needed.

He was thankful that it was the middle of summer – not winter. The house was immediately habitable and the beds were dry, even though fires had not been lit for a week. Before he left, he promised that their housekeeper, Mrs Robertson, who was a soul of discretion, would be despatched to meet their every need within the hour. Victoria, again filled with trepidation, was concerned at how the news would be received by his parents. He assured her he would return before the evening was over.

Having been transported back to the mansion house, Alexander finally dismissed the coachman, with a considerable bonus for his extra passengers, and went inside. He immediately sought out Mrs Robertson, fondly known as Robbie by the family, although no one ever dared address her as such.

'But the guest rooms are ready in the house, sir,' said Mrs Robertson, clearly surprised by his request to see to the comfort of a young lady and a child at the cottage.

'This is a special favour to me,' said Alexander persuasively, well aware that he had been a favourite with Robbie since he was a child. 'I would be obliged if you would see to the young lady's needs as discretely as possible.'

'I will see to it personally,' she assured him.

'I want to surprise my parents, you see.'

'I understand perfectly, sir.'

'Where are my mother and father, by the way?'

'Lady McNair is in her room, I believe. Your father will not be back before eight o'clock this evening. Dinner will be at eight-thirty.'

'Drat!' he exclaimed, while Mrs Robertson's shrewd old eyes narrowed curiously at his evident agitation. 'Never mind – thank you Mrs Robertson and remember this is between you and me.

'Of course, sir!'

He had planned to see his parents together and going upstairs, he was annoyed that his disclosure would now have to wait. His mother, however, met him on the upper balcony.

'So you're back,' she exclaimed, while he greeted her as usual with a kiss on her cheek. 'How was your visit?'

He was not prepared for this unexpected meeting and his mother immediately noted his discomfiture.

'What's wrong, Alexander?'

'I need to speak to you and Father on an urgent matter.'

'Urgent?'

'Don't be alarmed.'

'How can I not be, when you say it is urgent?'

He decided swiftly now; he could not delay.

'Let's go to your room.'

Rowena and David McNair had separate bedrooms connected by an adjoining door. Her room was an extensive L-shaped chamber, which had an area furnished with comfortable fluffy armchairs, a tea table, and a desk, where she dealt with her correspondence. As a child, Alexander had spent much time here being entertained by his mother and he took courage from the familiarity of the surroundings.

'I'm going to be married,' he revealed, as soon as they were seated.

'You found her!' exclaimed his mother, clapping her hands with delight. 'But this is wonderful!' Her joy was extinguished like a snuffed candle, however, by the continuing sobriety of his expression and she paused, hands caught in an attitude of prayer. 'There's something else?'

Alexander sat forward, his voice barely above a whisper, as he tried to cushion the shock of his news. 'I learned today I have a six-month-old son.'

'Wh . . . what?' Her face was a study of confusion. 'This . . . this cannot be.'

'I'm so sorry – I've let you down badly.'

'A grandson,' she whispered incredulously. Her hands which had remained in their prayer-like pose moved abruptly to cover her mouth, as the full enormity of his revelation struck her.

He moved from his chair to kneel before her and hold her wrists, while her hands pressed ever harder against her face, as if to stifle a scream. He bowed his head in helpless torment at her distress and for several minutes they remained thus, like statues immortalized in a moment of emotional drama.

When finally she came to life, he looked up again and saw the whole of the lower half of her face was whitened by the pressure she had exerted. Her mouth twitched several times, before she managed to ask huskily, 'Can you get me some tea?'

He hurried to the kitchen personally and, in due course, brought a tray up. By then, she seemed to have recovered somewhat, although she was frighteningly distant, as she rejected his help and poured the tea herself, despite the trembling of her jewelled hand.

After she had taken several sips of the hot sweet liquid, she asked, 'What kind of woman is she – to have allowed herself to be compromised in this way?' Her voice was laced with contempt. 'And to think, I encouraged you in tracing her!'

'It was not her fault. She was naïve and innocent. It was I, who took advantage.'

'So innocent, she has now trapped you!' retorted his mother disbelievingly. 'Can you even be sure the child is yours?'

'I can't have you speak of her like that,' he responded firmly. 'There is no doubt the child is mine and she is here because I sought her out – not because she was out to ensnare me.'

'Here?' echoed his mother, her voice spiralling in alarm. 'In our house?'

Even when he explained where he had left Victoria, his mother remained irate. 'How could you do this? How did you dare to bring her on to this estate before you even spoke to your father or me?'

'I could not bear to leave her and my son one minute longer in a godforsaken place in the middle of nowhere!' he retorted, for the first time anger colouring his tone.

'Who is this woman?' she demanded bluntly.

The name immediately triggered her memory.

'The daughter of Jeremy Liversidge!' she exclaimed. 'Good God, Alexander. It grows worse. David will. . . .' She raised trembling hands in the air, as words momentarily failed her. 'I simply cannot conceive of how he will react!'

'I recall you rather liked her father,' he pointed out, 'and you will like her, if you give her a chance.'

She looked aghast at such a prospect, but said nothing as she tried to assimilate all that she had learned. The fact that this girl was of their class was something, but for the scandal of her father's suicide to be topped now by this outrage was insupportable. Anticipation of the notoriety that her favourite son was about to inflict upon them finally demanded tears.

And it was thus Sir David found them, as he breezed in unexpectedly early – his wife weeping quietly, while Alexander sat holding his head in despair.

'What's wrong here?' he asked immediately, while his son stood up to face him and his wife, dabbing hastily at her eyes, looked at him fearfully.

Alexander did not waste words now, as he knew that prevarication could only prolong the agony. The information was delivered with all the verbal economy, he could muster and Sir David's reaction was equally swift. A vicious blow descended on the side of Alexander's face. He reacted instinctively. His right fist swung to within inches of his father's jaw, before his brain put on the brakes. His mother gasped and rose, as if to intervene, while Alexander stood, his whole body shaking from his effort of restraint.

'Perhaps, you were entitled to that,' he muttered hoarsely. 'But don't . . . don't *ever* do it again!'

'Please. . . .' His mother's voice whimpered between them, as they stood glaring at each other, like two gladiators.

Sir David's eyes flickered to his wife and he slumped suddenly into an adjacent chair, while Alexander slowly unbent his fists and relaxed every taut muscle in his body.

But he knew it was not safe to continue any discussion at the moment. He walked from the room without another word, intent only on ensuring that his mother was spared the wretched indignity of witnessing her husband and son brawling on the floor.

CHAPTER TWENTY-THREE

TWILIGHT was descending on the glen that night, as Mhairi-Anne, seated on farmer John Linton's cart, returned to the hunting lodge after her excursion to Perth. She had much to tell Victoria. Not only had the agent, recommended by Victoria's lawyer, sold the three of her paintings which Victoria had posted from Tora, he wanted more, and the sums involved, though modest, were encouraging. Although she had done no painting since leaving Tora and all of her other work remained there still – the prospect that she might one day earn a living through her talent was exciting and comforting. So far, they had managed financially, but they needed the long-term security of an income and she longed to see Victoria's face, when she showed her the money residing safely in her purse.

'Not far now,' said John, flicking his whip gently over the horse's rear, more by way of reassurance, than anything else. He was a kindly man, in late middle age, with two grown-up sons to share the load of work on the farm, which was increasingly too heavy for him. Thus, he generally worked on their market stall in Perth during the summer months – enjoying the banter of his customers – and a few jugs of ale afterwards, before he returned home. Without his help, by way of provisions and transport, the two women could not have managed life in the glen, but he had always had a soft spot for Victoria, who had been a regular visitor to the area with her father, as a child, and his suicide had only confirmed John's unconditional goodwill towards her, her widowed friend and the baby, who had been born during their stay.

'You seem to have had a good day at the market,' remarked Mhairi-Anne, glancing at the empty cart, which had been full of produce when he had collected her early that morning.

'Aye – the tatties went down a treat. Made a nice pile o' shillin's the day, I did. Have you been buyin' things for the bairn?' he queried, nodding at the pile of packages stacked at her feet.

She smiled fondly. 'He's growing so quickly, we can hardly keep up.'

'A fine little lad he is, too,' responded John approvingly. 'I have to hand it to you two lassies – managin' all on your own without a man about the place. His father would have been right proud o' him, no doubt.'

She nodded silently. The Lintons had apparently accepted unquestioningly their story that Alex's father had died, but she sometimes wondered if they suspected otherwise.

'There she is!' said John, as the outline of the lodge emerged in the distance, just as the rim of the sun disappeared behind the range of hills.

Mhairi-Anne held on to the side of the seat, as the road became rougher at this point and birds were startled into the darkening sky, squawking from their roosts in trees, as the cart-wheels trundled noisily over the pitted surface. The glen had blossomed in all its beauty under the summer sun and she knew that there was some fine scenery just waiting for an artist's brush, but, strangely, she had lost all urge to paint since leaving Tora and taking up residence in the lodge. She missed the island more than she had ever anticipated: the relentless noise of the sea; the aromatic smell of the peat; the defiant grandeur of rock and land in its subtle concoction of colours – all of which had never failed to inspire her to draw and paint. But now, she had a practical incentive to begin some new work and she had even bought the necessary implements that day, to get started immediately. Of course, Calum or James might be contacted, with regard to sending on the store of paintings residing on Tora, now that these could bring in some more money, but Victoria could hardly make such a request and they had never revealed that she was with her at the lodge, nor anything about the baby's birth. It sometimes worried her as to how long they might protect their secret, but, since leaving Tora, she had tended to live from day to day, trying desperately to forget the past and not anticipate the future.

'I wonder that Victoria has not lit the lamps,' she murmured now, as they approached slowly through the gloom, which remained unrelieved by any light from the hunting lodge.

'The bairn's probably been keepin' her busy,' responded John dismissively.' Daylight goes quick in these parts.'

She did not answer, as she watched the dark square of the lodge grow slowly before her eyes. A feeling of disquiet was gradually possessing her. Something was wrong. She knew it even before the cart trundled to a halt in front of the lodge gate and she stared worriedly at the dark windows.

'I'll wait, while you check,' said John, as Mhairi-Anne leapt down and hurried up the path, leaving her parcels behind.

The stout door opened immediately when she turned the handle, but she knew instantly that no one was there. No warmth or smell of food greeted her and, as she blundered inside in the darkness, she saw the dying coals of the fire in the grate – long since unattended. She called, nevertheless, as she fumbled for matches and lit the lamp on the table. The small parlour appeared before her eyes, as her voice continued to reverberate through the house. 'Victoria . . . Victoria . . . !'

Panic seized her, as she held the lamp aloft and hurried to the kitchen – then the bedroom, where Alex's crib lay still and empty, the covers thrown aside – the pillow frighteningly cold, as she touched the small indentation where his head had lain.

'Victoria . . .!' Her voice now reflecting her panic, spiralled, as she careered up the wooden stairs to the attic bedrooms. Nothing . . . no one.

John met her in the doorway, when she clattered back down the stairs.

'They're gone . . . gone . . . no one's here!' she muttered incredulously, her face paper-white with fear.

'Och – I bet we'll find her at the farm,' said John reassuringly. 'She'll have ta'en the bairn for a walk and then been too tired to make it back.'

Her face brightened at this idea, but only then did she notice the white envelope stuck in the letterbox.

'Wait a moment,' she murmured, snatching it free. There was no name on the outside, but, laying the lamp on an adjacent table, she ripped it open, her eyes devouring the brief lines:

Mhairi-Anne – no time to explain – I've had to leave suddenly with Alex. Book into The Swan Hotel in Perth. I'll contact you there as soon as possible. The key is on the mantelpiece. Leave it with John Linton after you lock up. Victoria.

'I think you'd better sit down, lassie,' said John, as she raised her eyes in shock and bewilderment. 'Bad news, is it?' he queried, as he encouraged her into the parlour, where she subsided, wordlessly, into the nearest chair. Glancing about for some means to revive her, he noticed a decanter of sherry on the sideboard and promptly poured a generous measure into a glass. 'Here – drink this.' He pressed the glass into her hand, which he then directed to her lips. 'That's it . . . you'll feel better in a minute.'

It was, in fact, several minutes, before she found the strength to speak, while John prattled on – a monologue of meaningless small talk – and resisted the temptation to take the offending epistle from the hand in which she had crushed it.

'She's . . . she's had to leave for some reason,' she murmured eventually. 'Here – read for yourself.'

He smoothed out the sheet and read as quickly as his limited powers of literacy and failing eyesight would allow. By this time, she had stood up to pace the room distractedly.

'I can't understand it – where can she have gone? It doesn't make any sense.'

'Must be a relation, I suppose,' ventured John. 'Someone's maybe died . . . or near dyin' . . . somethin' like that.'

'But she's never spoken of any of her relations – none of them wanted anything to do with her after her father's death. Why would they contact her now?'

'Well, someone must have come and got her from this place. Maybe the wife knows somethin'.'

'I doubt it,' she responded tightly, anger beginning to stir in her. 'She seems to have gone in a great hurry. How could she do this – knowing I'd be out of my mind with worry?'

'Have you checked what she's taken with her? Maybe that'll tell you somethin'.'

She immediately ran from the room to rifle drawers and cupboards, while he listened to the series of thumps and bumps, which reflected her progress. When she returned, her face was flushed with her efforts and tears stood grimly in her eyes.

'She's taken several of her own outfits and nearly all of Alex's things. . . .'

'Well then,' interjected John brightly, as she subsided weakly into the chair again, clearly fighting to control herself. 'If she's gone prepared, that's a good sign, isn't it? It's not as if she's been spirited off . . . unwillin', like.'

Extracting a handkerchief from her pocket, she blew her nose, shaking her head, as she did so. 'It just doesn't make any sense.'

'Maybe not now,' conceded the farmer soothingly, 'but if you go to The Swan as she says, chances are she'll turn up there tomorrow, right as rain, bairn an' all.'

She looked up, blinking rapidly. 'Do you think so?'

'Like as not, she will.'

She nodded uncertainly. 'She's bound to know how worried I'll be.'

' 'Course she will. That's settled then. You pack up your things and I'll pick you up again around dawn. I'll just keep your parcels on the cart, as you'll want them with you now, I suppose.'

'But you don't go to market tomorrow.'

'I can spare an hour – no bother.' He stood up. 'But I'll need to head on home, or my Peggy will be thinkin' I've downed too much ale and ended up in a ditch somewhere.'

She rose to walk with him to the door.

'Will you be all right now? You could come an' spend the night at the farm, y'know. Peggy would enjoy a chin-wag.'

'I'll be fine,' she assured him. 'Besides, I need to pack.'

He waved to her from the cart. 'If Peggy knows anythin' at all, lassie, I'll be back the night.'

As he trundled off into the consuming darkness, she closed the door and returned to the parlour. The dead fire underlined the abandonment of the place and she shivered as she poked the grey ashes, until she found a few red coals underneath, which she supplied with a few sticks. Seated on the coal-box, she watched as flames began to lick over the wood, to flicker eerily around the room so that shadows pulsated to the relentless question hammering at her brain. Where is she? Where is she? Where is she?

While the fire took hold, so, too, did a knot of fear in the pit of her stomach, growing like a cancerous tumour inside her. The idea of some mysterious relation turning up had given way to a much more credible possibility and even more unanswerable questions. Had Alexander McNair found them? Had he learned at last that he had a son? And, if so, why had Victoria complied with his abduction?

CHAPTER TWENTY-FOUR

AFTER the scene with his parents, Alexander immediately went to the stables, saddled the black stallion, and rode over to the cottage to see Victoria. He found her eating a meal that Robbie had transported to her, while Alex lay gurgling on a mat before the fire, which the housekeeper had also thought to light.

As, necessarily, he had to lie to protect her feelings, he did not remain long. The revelation, he told her, had gone as well as could be expected, and he was hopeful that his parents would support them. On the way back home, however, he was already wondering if he had enough money saved from his last year's allowance, to move abroad with Victoria and his child, and how he might possibly earn a living there. He felt sure that his father would never forgive him. There were other, far more worthy candidates among cousins on his mother's side, who might inherit Strathcairn. In a way, he could not blame him, if he were disinherited.

When he returned to his room, however, dinner forgotten, he found his father awaiting him. As he hesitated inside the doorway, assessing his mood, Sir David said gruffly, 'Sit down! We have to talk.'

Alexander took a seat across from his father, one of the two that straddled the fireplace.

'Now your mother's not here, let's be frank. This girl – how much will it cost to buy her off?' he demanded bluntly.

Alexander emitted a contemptuous laugh. 'I might have known you'd think money was the answer. How much to have a grandson disappear, eh?'

'Who's to know who fathered the child – a girl like that! Are you named on the birth certificate?'

'There is no birth certificate – yet. Due to the circumstances, she was attended only by a midwife – not a doctor – and she feared that if she attempted to register the child, giving my name as the father, this might cause interest. We are rather well known in these parts!'

'She probably didn't dare use your name, until you volunteered for the role,' scoffed the older man, not convinced.

'I know he's mine!' Alexander blazed at him. 'Credit me with some sense.'

'You can't possibly be sure,' Sir David blustered, disconcerted by his son's conviction. 'Her father's suicide could easily have unhinged her brain.'

'Yes – but it didn't, which is a testimony to her strength of character and integrity – something, dare I say – which we seem to lack in this family.'

'You do, at any rate!'

'Yes,' agreed Alexander wearily, 'but I'm trying to put that right by marrying the girl. I should have done so when it happened, but – as you say – I've been a bit lacking in the strength of character and integrity department.'

'The point is that it never should have happened, if *she* had behaved herself!'

'So, it's her fault now – not mine?' quipped Alexander, sarcastically.

'It's women that control these matters in the end. How many rakes your mother saw off, before me, I couldn't count on two hands.'

'Oh for God's sake!' Alexander exclaimed distractedly. 'We're almost into the twentieth century, but you're determined to see her as some kind of Jezebel.'

'Who's to say she's not played fast and loose with someone else?'

'If you knew the girl at all, you'd realize how idiotic that is. She's been living in a hunting lodge in the middle of nowhere for the past year and I am the child's father, as surely as you are mine – although, no doubt, you are sorely regretting that fact right now.'

'Let's assume the child is yours,' conceded Sir David, after a long pause. 'The point is – born out of wedlock – there will always be suspicion attached to him. You could marry any girl you choose and have other children.'

'I'm going to marry Victoria – with or without your approval.'

'And lose everything?'

'If you so wish!'

'You're a fool!' barked Sir David, standing up and glaring down at his son. 'I've had enough of your nonsense for tonight.'

Alexander remained silent, as his father strode angrily to the door and banged it shut behind him.

It was almost midnight and he was lying in his dressing-gown, on top of his bed, when he heard a light tap at his door, before it opened to reveal his mother, who was also ready for bed. She closed the door softly behind her and stood uncertainly, while he rolled into a sitting position.

'I couldn't sleep, thinking I have a grandson I have not seen,' she murmured.

He nodded. 'I can't sleep either.'

'Your father says you're set on marrying this girl?'

'Don't try to change my mind, Mother. I've never been more certain of anything in my life. It's not just because I have a child I want to see grow up. I owe her this.'

'I thought you loved her. Wasn't that why you looked her up in the first place?'

'Whether I love her or not, I'd still marry her in these circumstances,' he muttered evasively.

'What is the child like? Tell me.'

'As beautiful, as you would wish.'

She nodded wordlessly, before she said decisively, 'We must find a way. I'll speak to your father.' She put her arms out to him and he moved swiftly into her embrace.

'I'm sorry I've disappointed you,' he murmured against her cheek.

She squeezed his arm, as she looked up at him. 'I'm disappointed – yes – but the more I've thought about it, I think I'd have been even more disappointed had you given in to our pressure.'

Once Lady McNair had made up her mind to make the best of the situation, Sir David's opposition lost impetus and it was only a matter of days before he, too, yielded. After Rowena had faced the first awkward meeting with Victoria and seen her grandson, whom she declared as uncannily like Eric, as a baby, her husband's anger gave way to curiosity.

Isobel, too, proved to be an unexpected ally to Alexander, in winning over his father. She had greatly appreciated his kindness since Eric's death, but she was also astute enough to realize that it was upon Alexander that her long-term security at Strathcairn depended. Thus, she added her counsel to Rowena's, when Sir David dallied about the necessary meeting of his future daughter-in-law and his grandson. And once he saw his grandson, the date of the marriage was swiftly fixed.

Victoria might have been ecstatic, but for the terrifying, guilty knowledge that Mhairi-Anne was, undoubtedly, at this moment, awaiting her arrival at The Swan Hotel. Thus, as soon as she could arrange it, she contrived to make a visit to Perth, on the pretext that she needed to visit her lawyer, in order to arrange the sale of the hunting lodge – true enough in itself – but, in reality, a credible excuse to make the vital detour, on which her future depended.

'I'll come with you,' Alexander volunteered.

'I also want to make some purchases for my trousseau,' she

insisted. 'It will be very boring for you and – besides – I want to take my time.'

Alexander sighed. 'Women and shopping! I guess I would rather stay here, but perhaps, Mama or Isobel would like to accompany you.'

'Really Alexander – I hardly know them yet.'

He nodded agreeably and Victoria swallowed on a mixture of relief and terror.

Everything had worked out better than she could have hoped: everything, that is, concerning the McNair family. But she knew that ahead of her lay an even greater trial, which could not be avoided any longer: her meeting with the woman, whose child she had effectively stolen.

CHAPTER TWENTY-FIVE

THE five interminable days that Mhairi-Anne spent in The Swan Hotel in Perth, awaiting Victoria's promised contact, were a quiet nightmare, full of the silent psychological torment, which only the unknown can inflict. Her room was a prison of alternating fits of despair and anger, while she feared that any outing to alleviate the relentless tension might coincide with vital news – or even a visit.

Staff soon began to be intrigued by the mysterious woman in number nineteen, as she came to be known, as she ate little, tidied her own room and never ventured beyond its threshold. Most thought she was the victim of some passionate romantic entanglement. 'He must be married,' voices whispered, as they passed her perpetually closed door. The hotel manager began to fear for her safety and, more importantly, some scandal afflicting the reputation of his hotel, should she succumb to the private misery that everyone agreed was written all over her beautiful face. Thus, several times a day, he sent staff on bogus errands to her door, simply to ensure that she remained with the living.

Mhairi Anne, preoccupied with the terrible, all-consuming task of awaiting an event she feared would never happen, was largely oblivious to the speculation which grew around her. She lost weight; her complexion paled due to her internment; and navy-blue shadows blemished her eyes. Generally, she slept late in the mornings, as she had great difficulty falling asleep in the first place, after suffering another fruitless day of disappointment. When she awoke, there was always hope to buoy her. Today, there must be news, she always thought. Nights, however, were agony, with seemingly endless hours of darkness to be endured before any revival of her expectation that this ordeal might imminently be over with a simple knock at her door.

As she had requested a room to the front of the hotel, usually she sat on a chair by the window overlooking the entrance, where any carriages drew up. Not that there were many such arrivals during her stay. The Swan's main attraction was its proximity to the River Tay, with some rooms enjoying a fine panoramic view of the dark, fast-flowing waters, but it was a comparatively small establishment of no more than forty rooms and sometimes hours passed before any vehicle stopped at its doors. However, she watched not only for coaches, as she had concluded that Victoria might well send a messenger of some sort – or a letter – or arrive on foot. Consequently, all movements below her window were scrutinized and she came to know residents of the hotel merely by their regular comings and goings. Her heart always skipped a beat when she spotted any obvious stranger entering the place – only to be repeatedly disappointed, when no summons followed this excitement.

Some of the time she passed in attempting pencil sketches of Alex, from her memory of his chubby, endearing little face, but while the image remained crystal clear in her mind, a likeness remained constantly elusive. Several times, the frustration of this activity brought tears. If she did not see him again soon, would the image gradually fade in her mind, she wondered fearfully? At such moments, her despair was matched only by fitful rages against Victoria for subjecting her to such torment. Or was it Alexander, she should be raging against, she wondered? The problem of not knowing what had taken place inevitably added to the confusion of her feelings, as her mind vaulted from one possibility to another. Victoria had been her best friend, after all. Everything she knew of her suggested that she would not willingly have inflicted such anguish upon her. And yet, if Victoria had been a victim, it seemed that Alexander must be a villain, who had arrived out of the blue and forced his will upon her. In the waiting, there were only other questions – never finite answers.

In one of her darkest hours, the fact that she had formerly lost a child also rose to haunt her. She had never wanted Neil Graham's baby. Perhaps, losing Alex was to be her ultimate punishment for wishing away that other life within her and for the blasphemous relief she had felt, when James had told her after the fire, that she was no longer pregnant. As thoughts of the island crowded into her mind, she thought suddenly, too, of Calum. He was the only other person who knew of her affair with Alexander. How she needed his wisdom and his strength now, she thought desperately! On impulse, she sat down at the writing-desk and wrote a short, urgent letter to him, begging him to come to the mainland to help her. However, having gone to bed, determined to have one of the staff post the letter for her in the morning, she awoke the following day, hoping once more that soon her misery would be over and fearful that any such contact with Tora might only initiate unnecessary complications. After all, she was only surmising that Alexander was involved. There might be some other explanation, she told herself, as she resumed her post by the window.

Considering the number of hours she spent watching the entrance below, it was ironic that she did not actually see the Strathcairn coach arrive at the corner of the street, nor Victoria stepping down and walking along towards the hotel, looking up fearfully at the rooms above. She had broken her vigil to eat a light lunch by the fireside table, when the knock came lightly on her door. As one of the maids had just left after depositing her tray, she automatically assumed something had been forgotten and simply called out, 'Come in!'

When she saw Victoria standing on the threshold, the teaspoon she was holding slipped from her fingers to clatter noisily on to the tray below.

'Good Heavens! You've come at last,' she muttered breathlessly, her heart fluttering erratically, like a bird suddenly frightened inside her chest.

Victoria, resplendent in her best outfit – a fitted suit in chocolate brown silk with a wide flowing skirt – looked well, but was evidently as agitated as she, from the way her eyes darted around the chamber, avoiding hers.

But Mhairi-Anne was not at all interested in how the other woman *looked*. One startling, frightening fact had registered. 'Where is he?' she demanded rising to her feet.

'Safe and well.'

'Where . . . where?' Her voice rose, as it now dawned with terrible clarity that her ordeal was not over at all.

Victoria closed the door quietly behind her, but remained still some yards distant, as she said tremulously, 'He's . . . he's with his father . . . at Strathcairn.'

Although, in some ways, Mhairi-Anne's imaginings had prepared her for this revelation, as it had long seemed the only credible possibility, actual confirmation momentarily winded her. She sank back into her chair, her face blanching, while Victoria advanced to stand over her.

'Can . . . can I pour you some tea?' she asked nervously.

Mhairi-Anne glared up at her. 'Tea!' she echoed disbelievingly. 'My child has been abducted, you have betrayed me, and you offer me *tea*!'

Victoria sat down opposite, evidently steeling herself. This was only the beginning, she thought, and she could not afford to feel pity for her. 'Alexander did not abduct him – as you put it,' she informed her quietly, 'and I did not betray you in the way you seem to imagine.'

'He has my child at this very moment!' retorted Mhairi-Anne.

Victoria took a deep breath of courage. 'He believes Alex is my child.'

'Wh – what?'

'We had a . . . er . . . relationship on Tora.'

Mhairi-Anne gazed across the space which separated them, her expression aghast. 'I . . . I don't believe you.' Her voice was barely a whisper.

'I can assure you, it's true. When he came to the hunting lodge, Alex was asleep at first, but he awakened and cried out.'

The shock of this revelation seeping into her inexorably, Mhairi-Anne exclaimed, 'And you allowed him to assume that Alex was your child?'

For a moment, Victoria's eyes fled shamefully to the gloves she was twisting in her hands, before she looked up defiantly. 'Yes, I let him think that. So you see, I did not betray anything about you.'

'No, you did much worse,' suggested Mhairi-Anne, as her brain began to leap at the ramifications of all she had been told. 'You took my place and for what reason, I wonder. Has he asked you to marry him, by any chance?'

Victoria had no need to confirm this assertion. The sudden blush of colour in her cheeks told all.

'And you think you'll get away with this charade?' continued Mhairi-Anne incredulously.

'Whether I will or not depends on you.'

'How very astute you are! But do you imagine for one second that there is any doubt that I will be claiming my child, now I know definitely where he is?'

'Then you will ruin the life that I have opened up for him. As things are, he has already been accepted by the McNair family, with all that this means for his future. He has been united with the father you thought he would never know and I . . . I . . . am happy to be his mother.'

A cold fury swept over Mhairi-Anne. 'How dare you? How dare you try to use *my child* as a passport to marriage?'

'Alexander asked me to marry him on Tora. I refused then – believing he was in love with you.'

Again Mhairi-Anne was shaken to the core, her lips trembling wordlessly.

'But he never asked you to marry him, did he?'

Mhairi-Anne stood up, wrenching her eyes away from the taunting face of a woman, she realized now, she had never really known. Turning her back, she walked slowly to the window before she responded. 'Clearly, I was fooled by both you and Alexander,' she murmured.

'No more than we were fooled by you,' retorted Victoria. 'He could hardly marry his uncle's mistress, could he?'

Mhairi-Anne spun round. 'You hate me, don't you?'

'When you told me about your relationship with James McNair, I did,' Victoria admitted tightly.

'Yet you took me in . . . helped me.'

'You claimed you wanted away from Alexander – to spare him – but I'm afraid I did not believe you.'

'So you determined to keep watch over me – to save your lover from my terrible clutches?'

Victoria shrugged. 'I suppose I was wrong in that . . . and other things. I'm not doing this now because I still hate you.'

'No, your motives are utterly egocentric, are they not?'

'Not entirely. Believe it or not, I love Alex, too. Now I am in a position to secure his birthright; something you can never give him.'

Mhairi-Anne gazed across the room, realizing fully for the first time, the terrible nature of the choice which now faced her. 'What you have done is unforgivable!'

Victoria stood up, fumbling with her gloves, head down. 'I . . . I realize – truly I do . . . what a sacrifice I'm asking.' She looked up, eyes earnestly entreating. 'I would never have done this deliberately. You said, when you became James McNair's mistress that you felt you really had no other choice. That's how I felt in a way, when Alexander arrived that day. Of course, I could have told him the truth, but what would that have achieved?'

'He might just have asked me to marry him,' muttered Mhairi-Anne grimly.

'Yes, but at what cost?'

'You mean his parents would never have accepted me – a peasant schoolteacher – not to mention a former whore.'

'I've never called you that.'

'No, but you've thought it.'

'The point is, I have a chance of acceptance: you don't. Not if the truth were known.'

'And whereas a whole island might tell the truth about me – only I know the truth about you!' A travesty of a smile quivered over her lips. 'And if I spoke up, what a dreadful scandal that would be for the mighty McNairs: two women eligible to claim their grandson, who would, no doubt, end up a laughing stock!'

Victoria was guiltily silent. She had done this and there was no way back.

'I think you had better leave,' Mhairi-Anne said suddenly, her voice trembling with impotent rage and fear.

'I must know what you intend to do. . . .'

Her voice tailed to a halt, as Mhairi-Anne's eyes flashed dangerously. 'You claim you felt you had no other choice in this and threw back similar words I'd used about my relationship with James McNair. But the difference is – I've learned since then that we always have a choice: pretending we don't is the easy way out.'

Victoria's cheeks flushed pink. 'How will I know . . . ?'

'When I arrive to collect my child – you will know!' retorted Mhairi-Anne grimly, before deliberately turning her back once more, to gaze out of the window through a haze of unshed tears.

She heard the door close quietly; saw Victoria emerge below to walk swiftly away along the street towards a handsome black coach; realized with a heavy heart that, despite her defiant concluding words, before she could contemplate collecting her child from Strathcairn, she must make an agonizing decision, which, either way, would surely haunt her for the rest of her life.

In claiming Alex, she must destroy all the opportunities now open to him; in not claiming him – how could she go on living? And on top of this was the crushing knowledge of Alexander's certain duplicity. Perhaps this had been his punishment for James, she thought bleakly, or, perhaps, he was a lying scoundrel, who had never loved her at all. In any case, he could never have assumed Victoria had borne Alex, had he not been intimate with her. And now she might lose her child because of it.

It was like the judgement of Solomon, she realized despairingly, recalling the horror she had felt as a young child in Tora church, when she had first heard the frightening story of two women, who had come before the king – both claiming they were the mother of a baby. Like other children, she had cried out in protest at the king's decision to resolve the dispute by cutting the child in two with a great sharp sword and it had been such tales, with the focus always on the bloodthirsty elements, not the moral, that had contributed to her gradual disillusionment with the religious zeal and fanaticism of people like William Morrison. Similar to the mother in the story, who had been prepared to give up her child to the other woman, in order to save it, she could see with painful clarity that the sacrifice of her own love could only benefit Alex. He was too young to remember her . . . miss her. He would still have a mother and everything else she would wish for him, but only without her. Unlike the Biblical character, however, there was no hope that she could ultimately win her child back through unselfishly offering to give him up now; in making this sacrifice, she would lose him forever. The awful finality of this searing thought reduced her to her knees.

Much later that night, however, staff in The Swan were amazed to see Mhairi-Anne pass through the hotel foyer – an arresting figure in a pale-blue dress and matching bonnet, with the veil drawn down fully over her face – on her way out. As the door clanged shut behind her, voices rose excitedly behind the desk.

'She'll get a chill goin' out dressed like that at this time o' night. No shawl or anything – did you see her?'

'She must be goin' to meet 'im!' opined the other. 'The coach'll be round the corner, I bet.'

'Oh – I wonder who he is?' sighed the first.

'Did you know a woman came to see her the day?'

'Naw – I must have been off duty.'

'I took it to be *his* wife.'

'Oh my! I wonder when she'll be back.'

By midnight, Mhairi-Anne had not returned and the more senior of the two staff on duty behind the desk concluded that they must report this eventuality to the hotel manager, as soon as they saw him.

He waited until noon the following day, before reporting agitatedly to the police that one of his guests had vanished, bill unpaid.

CHAPTER TWENTY-SIX

WITH the wedding date fixed for 5 August, speed and secrecy were of the essence, Lady McNair insisted, if they were to minimize the scandal. Victoria and Alexander were, therefore, married quietly in the little church on the Strathcairn estate, with no prior formal announcement. Only the immediate family was present at the ceremony, with the exception of James and Calum – at Alexander's insistence.

Outside the church, however, servants, estate workers, tenant farmers and all their families, who had only been told of the event that morning, gathered to see the couple emerge as man and wife. Although the news had caused a sudden feast of gossip, Lady McNair was satisfied that it had been contained for the moment and she was surprised that Alexander's popularity was not diminished by the event. The cavalier nature of his marriage seemed to add spice to the romantic interest which had long followed him and the fact that he had 'stood by the girl', who had borne him a child, was regarded by most as commendable.

If expense had been saved on the wedding, none was spared on the gown that Victoria wore, the making of which Lady McNair had supervised personally. In pure ivory satin, its cut was classically simple, with a full skirt, which fitted tightly over her hips and a fashionable bodice incorporating long sleeves and a high collar. A chiffon yoke completed the broad-shouldered look, while tasteful trimmings of lace, ribbon, fringe and pearl embroidery, looped with chiffon lilies-of-the-valley made the dress a masterpiece in needlework. In his kilt, teamed with a dark-green velvet jacket, Alexander, too, looked striking and Victoria was aware of the many envious glances cast her way, as they walked the short distance from the church back to the house in showers of rose petals. She felt like a queen and thought repeatedly that this day might have been the happiest of her life, but for the fear that continued to haunt her every breath: the possible appearance of Mhairi-Anne. But surely, it was now too late, she thought, glancing at the gold band adorning her left hand, which was linked securely through Alexander's arm, as they proceeded along the uneven pathway from the church. She *must* have realized that she had nothing to gain in exposing her, while Alex had everything to lose. And, perhaps, even now, she was beginning to appreciate her freedom again. Without a child, she would be a much more attractive prospect to other men and it was certain that she would not be short of admirers, if she put her mind to it. These were comforting thoughts and, as they approached the front entrance to the mansion house, Victoria's heart lifted. She knew that she had done wrong in taking the child, but she and Alex were now part of this prestigious family and, ultimately, her action would surely prove justified.

At the celebration luncheon which followed, James showed his evident pleasure in the union, but it was Calum, whom Alexander wanted to see alone. Finally, while Victoria changed prior to their departure on an extended honeymoon, he caught him by the window, looking out on to the lush gardens.

'Could we take a stroll, Calum?' He opened the French window on to the paved terrace.

As soon as they had moved beyond earshot, Alexander said, 'You must think I'm a liar and a rake, Calum, after all you went through with me on Tora and now you find I have a son to Victoria.'

Calum shrugged,'You don't need to worry yourself about my opinion, laddie. I know James was pushin' the two of you together. These things happen.' He paused before adding, 'I'm hopin', though, you'll be faithful to that lovely young wife of yours now. How did your parents take it?'

'Dreadful, at the beginning, but I think Alex saved the day. According to my mother's grandiose scheme for minimizing the scandal, we've to vanish abroad now for all of nine months. On our return, the grandson will be announced to the world, *fait accompli*, and Mother reckons that nobody will have the effrontery to comment on the fact that he'll be over a year old by that time.

'How will your father manage while you're away?'

'Fortunately, I've been urging him over the past year to get some good men in place to lessen the burden of control on us. Eric was always against relinquishing any power, but I see it as the only sensible way ahead, given Tora will also come to me one day. So, with all the new men, he won't be too hard pushed without me, I hope.'

'Alexander! Victoria is ready,' a voice called from the open window behind them.

He glanced back to the house to see his mother beckoning to him.

'Looks like I'm off on honeymoon.'

'Good luck and happiness to you.'

'Thanks, Calum,' said Alexander, as they shook hands. 'Just before we go in – I take it you've never heard anything of her – I mean – Mhairi-Anne?' The name stuck guiltily in his throat and Calum realized instantly, it was not really a question – more a statement which sought reassurance.

Thus, he shook his head solemnly, knowing there was no point in revealing now the contents of a letter he had received only the day before.

Alexander nodded and smiled, although he glanced away evasively.

Shortly, embroiled in farewells to everyone, including a tearful scene with his mother and an equally emotional parting from his father, Alexander had no further time to dwell on what might have been. Isobel, too, was upset and he had to spare a moment to give her a brotherly hug, before he and Victoria hurried to the waiting coach through another deluge of rose petals.

As the vehicle bowled away along the driveway, the cries of good wishes from the family were gradually swallowed by the rhythmic crunching sound of the wheels and, her arm linked through her husband's, Victoria settled her head comfortably on his shoulder, happy to allow exhaustion to overtake her. Now, it really was too late! They would not be back at Strathcairn for many months and, by that time, Alexander would surely have learned to love her.

Alexander, meantime, rested his head on the padded seat, as feelings of relief and resignation permeated his body, while the sight of his son, sleeping securely strapped to the other seat in the coach reassured him that he had done the right thing: the only thing. His obsession with the past had surely now been resolved; in time he would forget; in time he would be renewed. As the coach jogged them inexorably away from Strathcairn, he glanced down to see his wife had fallen asleep against his shoulder. Resolutely, he, too, closed his eyes and banished the tentacles of bleakness, which still gripped his heart.

The future awaited them. . . .